STARK REVENGE

A BASTARDS AND BADGES NOVEL

ANDI RHODES

Copyright © 2020 by Andi Rhodes

All rights reserved.

No part of this book may be reproduced in any form or by any electronic or mechanical means, including information storage and retrieval systems, without written permission from the author, except for the use of brief quotations in a book review.

Cover Artwork – © 2020 L.J. Anderson of Mayhem Cover Creations

For my dad, who has always encouraged me, supported me, loved me. I will forever be a daddy's girl. Please remember that when you read anything I've written ;)
Love you, dad.

ALSO BY ANDI RHODES

Broken Rebel Brotherhood

Broken Souls

Broken Innocence

Broken Boundaries

Broken Rebel Brotherhood: Complete Series Box set

Broken Rebel Brotherhood: Next Generation

Broken Hearts

Broken Wings

Broken Mind

Bastards and Badges

Stark Revenge

Slade's Fall

Jett's Guard

Soulless Kings MC

Fender

Joker

Piston

Greaser

Riker

Trainwreck

Squirrel

Gibson

Satan's Legacy MC

Snow's Angel

Toga's Demons

Magic's Torment

> "And in the middle of my chaos,
> there was you."
> **~Paullina Simons**

1

JACKSON

"Can I get you another?"

The half naked waitress leans over my table, her perky breasts pushed up by the corset she's wearing. The globes of her ass, not covered in spandex, are held in by fishnet stockings. I'm sure she was beautiful at one time, but now she just looks like she's been rode hard and put up wet.

"I'm good, Dee." I lift my glass and the inch of amber liquid that remains sloshes around the clinking ice. "Thanks."

I smile at her, hoping she gets the message that I want to be left alone. I like Dee, she's smart, friendly, accommodating, but she's been trying to get in my pants for a year now and I'm over it.

Normally, I'd fuel the fire, so to speak. It's my job, after all, to blend in. I've taken a waitress home a time or two. I've even paid for the club extras. I'm a man who likes to fuck, and I'm not ashamed to do something about it.

But not tonight. Tonight, I need to keep my wits about me and my dick in check. Besides, Kitty Kat's about to go on, and I definitely don't want to miss that. Over the last forty-one days, I've been eyeing her, sure that she's the key to this whole thing. It doesn't hurt that she's also the only stripper in the joint who doesn't seem to fit in.

Katelyn Dawson—stage name Kitty Kat—is five foot tall, with honey colored hair and hazel eyes. Her driver's license has her listed as an organ donor for fuck sake. She comes from a normal suburban upbringing and has a degree in special education. I know everything there is to know about Katelyn. Everything but why she's here, at The White Lily, wearing a black wig and taking off her clothes for filthy men.

When she steps on the stage, I almost wish I were sitting closer tonight and not in the dark corner where I can't offer any protection. The crowd is rowdier than normal, and the catcalls that ring out when she bends over, her perfect ass pointing up like a beacon for all fucked up men, has me gripping my glass so tight I fear it will shatter.

"C'mon Kitty Kat!"

"Shake that ass."

"Purr for me, baby."

Everyone is screaming, and I slide my gaze to the side door where I know he'll be standing. He doesn't look happy for a guy who has his best girl on stage and will no doubt be raking in the dough. His arms are crossed over his chest, and to some, he may be intimidating, but to me he's just a giant douche.

Kevin Vick, owner of The White Lily and the sole reason for me being undercover, is pissed. And Katelyn Dawson, stripper extraordinaire, girl next door, the cause of my painful boner, is the key to cracking the case.

I just have to figure out why.

He glances in my direction, and an evil smile forms. It's almost time for our weekly meeting. I throw back the rest of my Whiskey and slam the glass on the table before standing and making my way to the door that opens into the hallway lined with offices, where *business* is conducted.

Kitty Kat finished up a few minutes ago, and I really wanted to try to talk to her, but she'd been escorted off the stage by Jett and Stoner, two of Mr. Vick's most loyal enforcers. I've gotten to know both of them pretty well, and while Jett is pretty low-key, more muscle than brains sometimes, Stoner is batshit crazy. Since starting this gig, I've worked my way up, and I'm usually in charge of assigning protection, but Mr. Vick took a special interest in Kitty Kat from day one.

I walk through the doorway, down the dimly lit hall. On the surface, The White Lily is your run of the mill strip club, but dig a little deeper and you'll find the inner workings of the biggest drug ring in Indianapolis. That's why I'm here, what brought me undercover. At least that's the reason on the surface. Some days I feel like I'm living every lawman's dream and others, I'm so disgusted by it all that I wish I was back in my little rinky-dink town as the local sheriff.

But I'm not a sheriff any more. I'm Jackson Stark, fucking FBI agent, pretending to be Jack Duffy, head of security for Mr. Vick and his cronies. It didn't take me long to prove myself to Mr. Vick—a carefully crafted identity and backstory, a few drug buys, one or two displays of my skills, and I was in. Oh, and sabotaging his former head of security hadn't hurt.

It seemed like we were getting close to a bust. Everything was falling into place and then Katelyn started. Mr. Vick wouldn't let me anywhere near her, so of course, I got curious. I begged my superiors for more time. They'd wanted to make the arrest, bring the ring down, but something wasn't right. They gave me two months, but judging by Mr. Vick's attitude tonight, it might not take that long.

The closer I get to his office, at the end of the long hallway, the more my skin crawls. Like it always does when I have to be near him. The sound of muffled voices reaches me, and it isn't long before I hear one that doesn't belong. Usually these meetings are just Mr. Vick and me, maybe an enforcer or two, but there are never women. Ever. So hearing one now makes my stomach drop and has me reaching for the gun in my waistband.

The door is open a crack, and I see Katelyn sitting in a chair, with her arms and legs fastened to it with handcuffs. Her back is ramrod straight but she's sniffling, like she's been crying. Her hair is a mess and there is no sign of Kitty Kat, other than her lack of clothing. Not quite sure what's going on, I flatten myself to the wall so I can listen.

"Please, Mr. Vick, give me a few more days."

"I've given you more than adequate time, don't you think? Certainly more than our original deal."

Adequate time for what?

"Yes, sir, you've been very generous, but—"

The sound of a fist connecting with flesh has me stifling a groan. Everything in me is screaming to barge in and save her, but I know that would be a rookie mistake and the undoing of all my hard work.

"Now, Kitty Kat, you know I don't like to get my hands dirty, so why must you make me?"

The sound of a chair scraping across the floor has me chancing a peek through the crack, and I see Mr. Vick step up behind Katelyn and drape his arms over her shoulders to grab her breasts. While he's squeezing her hard enough to leave bruises, he leans in and whispers something in her ear.

When she shudders and I hear her whimper, I've had enough. Fuck the case and fuck my job. I can't stand by and watch him do this to a girl, no matter what deal with the devil she's made.

I push open the door and step through, schooling my features so that my anger and disgust don't show. All eyes turn to me and rage flows through me at the sight of Katelyn's face. Her eye is swelling shut, and there's mascara streaking down her cheeks from her crying. Blood is dribbling down her chin from her split lip.

She looks scared, but there's also a hint of something else. Something I wasn't expecting from this girl who doesn't belong in this world. There's a spark of defiance. It's evident in the way she juts her chin and maintains her stiff posture. She knows who I am and what I do for Mr. Vick. Most in her position would be quaking with fear, but not her. If I'd been drawn to her before, it was nothing compared to the magnet pulling me in now.

"Mr. Vick, I see the party started without me."

I casually stroll to stand next to his desk, shoving my hands in my pockets as I do. Jett and Stoner glare at me, and Mr. Vick bristles at having been interrupted.

"Well, now, Jack, the party has just begun." Mr. Vick gives Katelyn's tits another squeeze before he steps away and focuses his attention on me. He sweeps his hand to indicate the bloody woman and says, "Care to have a go at her? I've noticed the way you watch her up on the stage, all hot and bothered, and she's not going to be around much longer so…" He shrugs.

I have no interest in forcing myself on her or whatever else he means by 'have a go at her', but I'm not stupid either. Maybe this is my chance. Not only to get the information I know she has to put Kevin Vick away for good but also to figure out what it is about her that has me tied up in knots. I have to play this exactly right to be able to do either.

"She's not really my type." She's exactly my type, or more accurately, she's exactly what my type was before this fucking assignment.

"Good. Then I don't have to waste any more time on her. You've been an excellent employee and I thought you could use a reward, but since you're not interested, I'll let Jett and Stoner—"

"I never said I didn't want her," I interrupt, not liking where things are headed. "She may not be my type, but she's got a pussy and tits so maybe she can scratch an itch."

I hate how easily those words roll off my tongue. This job has changed me, made me into a man I hardly recognize sometimes. Deep down, I know I'm not going to hurt her, but there's a little part of me that wants what Mr. Vick is offering. The opportunity to lose myself between her thighs and walk away after I'm satisfied.

"Mr. Vick, this was never part of the deal," Katelyn yells. Splotches of red appear beneath the blood and mascara on her cheeks. She bucks wildly against the cuffs. "You promised that I—"

Stoner fists a hand in her hair and yanks her head back so he can wrap his other hand around her throat. When he applies pressure, her eyes widen and tears gather at the corners. Mr. Vick moves to stand in front of her and bends down so he's in her face, only inches separating them. He grabs her chin, and the skin around his fingers whitens under his grip.

"Listen up, little girl," he snarls. "You're in my world now and promises don't mean shit here. Understand?"

She tries to nod but it's made impossible by the two men holding her.

"I can't hear you."

"Y-yes," she stammers.

"Good." He shoves her face away and stands to his very unimpressive full height. "Now, are you going to be a good little reward for Mr. Duffy, or do Jett and Stoner need to take care of you instead?"

Katelyn's eyes dart back and forth between me and the two enforcers, as if weighing her options. She has no idea that I'm the safer bet, but I'm praying that Jett and Stoner scare her more than I do. When her gaze finally lands on me and stays there, I hold my breath. Silent tears fall as her lids slide closed.

In that moment I know that she's made her choice.

2

KATELYN

This can't be happening. I'm supposed to be teaching, helping young children with special needs learn what five plus three is, not having to choose between rape and death.

"I've got one condition."

My eyes snap open at the sound of Mr. Duffy's voice, and I lock eyes with him, terrified of what he's going to say.

"And what's that?" Mr. Vick asks, bristling.

"My kinda kink requires privacy." Mr. Duffy winks at me before turning to focus on Mr. Vick. "I'd much rather play with my reward where I don't have to worry about someone walking in and interrupting my fun."

Mr. Vick looks at me and his gaze lowers to my exposed breasts before returning his stare to Mr. Duffy.

"I need her back in one piece." He huffs out a disgusted laugh. "For some strange reason, I like her. And she still has a deal to fulfill."

"What deal is that, sir?"

"That's none of your concern, Jack." He waves an absent hand at me. "Take her and go."

Mr. Duffy hesitates for only a second before he comes to the chair and unlocks the cuffs. My body tenses, bracing for whatever he's about to do. He surprises me though and scoops me up in his arms, his touch incredibly gentle. As he carries me to the door, Mr. Vick's voice stops him in his tracks.

"And Jack?" Mr. Duffy stiffens, and when I look at his face, I see his eyes roll. "Make sure that any *marks* can be covered up. I don't want to have to take her debt out of your ass."

Mr. Duffy gives a curt nod and continues out of the room. The hallway is cold and I shiver, goosebumps covering my skin. He looks down at me and frowns before he sets me on my feet and takes off his worn leather jacket and wraps it around my shoulders. I don't know whether to thank him or run now that I'm free.

"Running wouldn't be wise, but I can think of several ways you can thank me." He smirks and I shrink back against the wall. He heaves a sigh and shoves his fingers through his black hair. "Believe it or not, I just saved your ass."

My temper spikes, and I clench my fists at my sides.

"Well excuse me for not trusting you."

He flattens his hands against the wall on either side of my head and leans in close to my ear.

"Ah, Kitty Kat, you'll learn to trust me. So much so that you'll crave what I have to offer." His breath skitters across my skin, and it sends tingles down my spine.

His cell phone dings, and he pulls it out of his pocket and looks at the screen.

"Shit." He grabs my arm and tugs me back in the direction we came. "Don't stop moving, no matter what you hear." His words are terse, etched with grit and determination.

He stops right before passing Mr. Vick's office door. He peeks in and apparently he's satisfied with what he sees because he yanks me past in a hurry and shoves open the rear exit door. The alarm blares as he drags me through the alley. I start to dig in my heels. I have no idea where he's taking me, and the thought of running from him is sounding more and more appealing.

Gunshots ring out from inside the building, and he increases his pace. The air is frigid, and my lungs are burning from trying to keep up with him. I can see the main street, and I scream, praying that someone will hear me, save me.

He flings me against the brick building and slaps a hand over my mouth.

"Are you fucking crazy?"

I struggle to breath and claw at his arm. His eyes drop to my fingers, and for a brief second, I think I see regret in them, but it doesn't last. He hardens his features and looks me right in the eyes.

"I'll take my hand away but no more screaming. Got it?"

I nod frantically, still struggling against his hold. When he drops his hand and steps back, I double over and rest my hands on my knees. I'm coughing, trying to suck in air. When I catch my breath, I straighten up and notice the grin on his face. He's trying hard to not laugh at my obvious discomfort, and his sick enjoyment flips a switch in me.

My palm connects with his cheek, and despite the sting, it feels incredibly satisfying. It'd be more satisfying if he had the decency to look like it hurt, even a little, but no. His grin widens and a dimple appears.

"Feel better?"

"Fuck you." I cross my arms over my chest and realize that I may have his jacket covering my shoulders, but my boobs are still on display.

His expression sobers, and when he reaches toward me, I flinch. He holds his hands up in a gesture of surrender.

"I'm just trying to cover you up," he says before he slowly

lowers his hands and grabs the bottom of his jacket and latches the zipper so he can tug it up.

That simple act is all it takes to open the dam. Tears well in my eyes, and the events of the last hour catch up to me. He pulls me toward him and wraps his arms around me, rubbing my back as I cry.

"I know you don't trust me, and I know you probably need to let loose and cry for hours, but I'm gonna need you to pull yourself together. You can break down later."

His voice is calmer than before, and there's no grit in it. He actually sounds kind, which is completely unexpected. I push away and peer up at him. He wipes the tears from my cheeks with the pad of his thumb and his smile is sad, not evil or scary like before.

I manage to pull myself together and let him lead me to a vehicle. I stand by the back driver's side door but he urges me around to the front passenger side. He helps me in and buckles my seatbelt, like I'm some fragile flower that can't take care of herself. Maybe I am. I've certainly gotten myself in a jam that I have zero idea how to get out of.

He turns the key, and the engine comes to life. As he pulls away from the curb, cop cars surround the building, and I can't help but stare at what could have been my rescue. Instead, I'm stuck with this guy, who is as confusing as he is scary.

"What the fuck, Slade?"

Mr. Duffy is pacing back and forth in the living room of the rundown house he brought me to. When we arrived, he helped me inside and immediately shoved me down on the couch with orders to 'stay' before he pulled out a cell phone from a drawer in the desk across the room.

"Goddammit! Everything's fucked now. No way do they have enough to hold him. He's gonna get out like the hundreds of other times, and I'm gonna have to handle the fallout."

As he paces, I can't help but notice the ways his jeans hug his thighs or the way his ass fills out said jeans. I can't help but see the way his black T-shirt stretches across his chest or the way his biceps seem to bulge beneath the sleeves.

"She could've been killed! Do you have any idea how lucky we are that I was able to get her out?"

His pacing stops and he settles on the arm of the sofa next to me. For some strange reason, I don't move. My brain screams at me to put some distance between us, but my body doesn't obey. He glances down at me with eyes that are hard, cold orbs of frustration.

"Fine. But I'm not bringing her in. Not yet." With that, he stabs the phone with a fingertip and ends the call. "Jesus, this isn't what I signed up for," he mumbles, more to himself than to me.

I'm curious as to his meaning but now that he's not distracted by his call, terror returns and I scurry to the other end of the sofa. He heaves a sigh as he stands and heads toward the kitchen.

"Can I get you anything to drink?" he calls over his shoulder.

A bottle of Tequila to drown my troubles in.

I don't say anything. If he thinks I'm going to make this easy on him, he's got another thing coming. He returns to the sofa and sinks down next to me. He hands me a bottled water, and when I don't take it, he sets it on the coffee table.

"Suit yourself." He takes a swig of his water, downing half of it in one go. After he screws the cap back on, he turns to face me. "Look, Katelyn—"

"How the hell do you know my name?" I only ever go by

Kitty Kat at the club. Mr. Vick is the only one who knows my real name, and keeping that a secret was part of our deal. Or so I thought.

"I know a lot about you... Katelyn Dawson." The way he says my name, how it rolls off his tongue like it's his favorite thing, is troubling. "For instance, I know you're twenty-six years old, you grew up in perfect suburban America, your parents are Lyle and Connie, you have a younger brother, Kyle, and you want to be a special education teacher."

"How... He said—"

"What I don't know, darlin', is why the *fuck* you work at The White Lily."

3

JACKSON

The look on Katelyn's face is killing me. A mixture of terror, confusion, and pain with a hint of I-wanna-fuck-this-guy. Jack Duffy, muscle for evil, wants to act on the latter, but Jackson Stark, widower and man with a conscience, wants to hold her and promise her that everything is going to be okay. I do neither of those things.

"C'mon." I grab her hand and pull her from her perch on the couch to the bathroom.

She doesn't dig in her heels completely, but she does resist a little. I flip on the light and urge her down on the closed toilet seat lid. Katelyn watches me warily from hazel eyes. I don't know whether to be flattered that she seems to like what she sees or worried that I'm so convincing as my undercover persona that she's still terrified I'm going to hurt her.

"You can relax. I'm not going to hurt you." I show her each item as I pull them out of the medicine cabinet and drawers: cotton balls, antibiotic ointment, butterfly bandages, hydrogen peroxide. "I just want to clean up your face."

Katelyn is wringing her hands in her lap, and when her tongue darts out to lick her lips, she winces at the sting of the nasty cut. The blood that was dribbling earlier has dried and is starting to crust. I know that me cleaning her up isn't going to feel pleasant, but it can't be helped.

"Why?"

"Why what?" I ask.

"Why are you being nice? If you're gonna rape me, I'd rather you just get it over with."

She turns her face away when I try to dab at the cuts with a peroxide soaked cotton ball. I grip her chin with my free hand, a little rougher than necessary, and force her to look at me and hold still.

"Jesus, I told you, I'm not going to hurt you. Now, quit being difficult."

I press the cotton to her face and dab at the dried blood. Air hisses through her clenched teeth, but she quits trying to pull away. Once I have her all fixed up, I pull a clean towel out from under the sink and hang it over the bar on the wall. Next, I step to the shower and turn the water on, adjusting the knobs to get the right temperature.

"While you wash up, I'll get you something to wear." I let my gaze travel the length of her body. "My clothes will swallow you up, but it's better than what you've got on."

She glances down at herself and her eyes widen as if she just now realized she's still half naked. When her gaze cuts back to me, her eyes narrow.

"I don't need a shower. I'm fine."

Her defiance is back, and I have to admit, it's kind of adorable. I like her better with a little fight in her. It doesn't hurt that it makes it easier for me to remember that I can't touch her. No matter how much I want to.

"Darlin', you smell like a bar full of puking drunks. You're getting in that shower one way or another." She eyes me warily but makes no move to get up off of the toilet and into the shower. "Fine, have it your way."

I scoop her up and deposit her under the spray, clothes and all. Her mouth hangs open until it starts to fill with water, causing her to sputter.

"What the he—"

"You've got five minutes. I suggest you don't waste them."

With that, I turn and walk out of the bathroom, leaving the door ajar. I grab a pair of sweatpants and a grey T-shirt from my bedroom. They'd been on the floor, so I sniff them and satisfy myself that they're clean. I go back and put the clothes on the bathroom vanity.

Katelyn is still in the shower, and she's muttering, clearly pissed off. Her stripper outfit, if one could call it an outfit, is slung over the shower curtain rod and I hear the click of a bottle lid being snapped shut.

I smile to myself as I exit the room and lean against the wall outside the door with my arms crossed over my chest. She's got spunk, I'll give her that. After a minute, I hear the water shut off and the rustle of the curtain being thrown open. It takes every ounce of willpower not to lean around the doorframe and get a look at her naked body.

The sound of her rustling through the cabinets has me shaking my head. When a drawer slams shut, I know she's found the unopened box of rubbers. My eyes widen when I hear the drawer slowly being pulled open again. Curious little thing.

I see her shadow before I see her. When she steps through the doorway, she looks to her right and, seeing nothing, turns to her left and runs into me. I grab her arms to steady her and notice that she's trembling. Her hand goes to her chest, and she struggles to catch her breath.

"Darlin', breathe." I bend at the knees and look into her eyes. "I didn't mean to scare you."

Apparently, me being nice is all it takes for her to snap back to spunky mode. She yanks out of my hold and juts her chin.

"You didn't scare me."

She crosses her arms over her chest. Kitty Kat on stage is sexy, but Katelyn, drowning in my clothes and hair wet and dripping, is fucking temptation personified. Add in the defiant pout and the sparkling eyes, and I'm almost wishing I wasn't such a decent guy. Almost.

"I scared you. But that's okay. I want you scared. It'll make you more cooperative." I grip her arm just above her elbow and steer her toward my bedroom. "I just don't want you scared of me."

We're standing in the middle of the room, and she's staring at the bed, with it's rumpled sheets. I'm just behind her and when she peers over her shoulder at me, I can practically see the wheels turning, wondering what is going to happen next.

"Have a seat." I nudge her toward the bed, and she takes an involuntary step forward, but that's it. "Oh, for fuck sakes."

I stomp to my dresser and open the top drawer. I dig around until I find what I'm searching for and grip it in my hand. My head is screaming at me to stop, to not blow this, but my heart dies a little more each time she shows fear. Besides, this operation is already blown nine ways to hell, so what more do I have to lose.

I step around her and flash my badge. "Feel better?" I snarl.

Her eyes grow round, and she snatches the badge from my hands. She inspects it, her gaze going back and forth between the shiny metal and my face.

"You're a—"

"An FBI agent." I shove my fingers through my hair and

begin to pace. "Do you believe me now? I'm not going to hurt you."

When she doesn't respond, I stop pacing and face her. Her face is pale and the purpling bruises are a stark contrast to the ghost white of her skin. Even from a slight distance, I can see that she's trembling harder than she was before, and confusion settles in at her reaction. She was supposed to relax with this knowledge, not become more frightened.

She tosses the badge onto the bed and turns to flee. I'm stunned and it takes me a second to follow. I reach her just as her hand twists the knob on the front door, finding it locked. I slam my hand on the wooden barrier and spin her around to face me. There are tears streaming down her cheeks, and she swipes at them as she averts her gaze.

"What the fuck, Katelyn? This should be good news. You don't have to go back there. You're safe, just like I promised." I hope it's a promise I can keep.

"You don't get it."

She shoves against my chest, and when I don't budge, she ducks under my arm. I whirl around to follow her movement. She's the one pacing now. Angry little steps, back and forth, back and forth. Her lips are moving, but I can't hear a word, although I can tell by the look on her face that she's pissed.

"Care to enlighten me?" Something about her reaction has a ball of dread forming in the pit of my stomach.

"Oh, what the hell?" she mutters before coming to stand in front of me. "You wanna know why I'm not happy? Why you being an FBI agent isn't the great revelation you were hoping it would be?"

This is not the reaction of a woman that was just saved by a knight in shining armor. I'm not sure I *want* to know, but I *have* to know.

"Yes." That one word comes out sounding more like a question than an answer.

"I'm not happy, asshole, because you just sealed my fate. In your rush to play the hero, you've signed my damn death warrant."

And with that, her knees buckle and she collapses to the floor and sobs.

4

KATELYN

This can't be happening. I'm so close and in the span of a few hours, the prize was ripped from me in epically horrible fashion.

"Katelyn, please, talk to me."

When his hand touches my arm, I lash out. I take a swing and rather than connecting with my target, my wrist is grasped in a vice-like grip.

"Not happening darlin'." There's no anger in his voice, only cocky confidence.

Sobs continue to tear out of me, and I struggle to suck air into my lungs. I try like hell to stop, to even out my breathing, but it doesn't work. Instead, it becomes more difficult, and I start to hyperventilate.

I'm lifted off the floor, and I can't even fight it. I have nothing in me left to fight with. My body is jarred when he sits down on the couch, cradling me against him. He strokes my hair, whispers reassurances in my ear. After what feels like hours, my breathing begins to even out.

"Good girl. Just breathe."

He never loosens his hold but somehow, it's not scary. It's

not forceful, and I don't feel trapped. His body heat, his deep voice, his constant touch... it's overwhelming, and oddly enough, exactly what I need. I let my head drop to his shoulder, and his scent curls around me. I can't describe it but I know it's all *him*.

"I'm really going to need you to explain." His breath skitters across my neck as he speaks and I shiver. "Are you cold?" He reaches behind him and pulls the blanket from the back of the couch and tucks it around me.

"Th-thank you," I mumble against his chest.

"You're welcome." He sits there for a few more minutes before he shifts and sets me on the cushion next to him. He may not be holding me in his lap, but now he has his fingers laced with mine, like he's afraid to let me go.

I take a deep breath and hold it for a few seconds before pushing it out. He's not going to just let me go, so I know I need to give him an explanation. I don't want to, but at this point, what choice do I have? Knowing it's over for me is one thing, resigning myself to the fact that my predicament will bring hell upon my family is something else entirely.

"Before I tell you anything, I need to know that you'll protect my family. My parents and my brother."

"Katelyn, that's not how this works."

I pull my hand out of his and cross my arms over my chest.

"Then do whatever it is you have to do to me in order to maintain your cover. I won't out you, but I'm not budging unless I know that he can't get to them."

This is probably a horrible play, but it's all I have and I'm banking on the fact that he wants to bring Kevin Vick down more than he wants to save me. He stares at me with hard eyes for a minute before reaching into his pocket and pulling out his cell phone.

"What are you doing?" I ask, panic evident in my tone.

"Getting another agent to figure out protection for your family," he says as he lifts the device to his ear.

"No!" I yell and lunge at him, grabbing for the phone before the call goes through.

He pulls it out of my reach, and we stare each other down as a voice comes through the line. I know I seem like a crazy person, stopping him from doing exactly what I demanded but I can't help it.

"Stark! Stark, man, talk to me. Are you okay?" The voice on the other end of the call is harsh, demanding. "Stark!" the voice shouts.

"Please," I whimper and my body seems to crumble. I hang my head and take a deep breath. "Please don't do this." When I hear nothing, I raise my head and see his eyes have softened and he's bringing the phone back to his ear.

"Sorry, Slade. Butt dial."

He disconnects the call and tosses his cell on the coffee table. The sound of it hitting the wood startles me, and I nearly jump out of my skin.

"You have five minutes to convince me that I just did the right thing by lying to my partner."

I open my mouth several times to speak, but no words come out. How is it possible that just a few minutes ago, this guy was comforting me, soothing me with his words and his touch, and now he looks like he wants to strangle me? Finally, I'm able to push words out.

"He called you Stark. I thought your name was Jack Duffy."

He laughs but there's no humor in it. "Darlin', I'm an undercover agent, do you honestly think Jack Duffy is my real name?"

"Well, no." I shrug and he shakes his head in disgust. "Look, this isn't exactly the life I'm used to living. Stripping, criminals, undercover agents, none of it is normal to me. I'm sorry if it's taking me a bit of time to adjust."

"Aw, I don't know about that. You seem pretty comfortable on the stage, Kitty Kat." He smirks and suddenly, I'm back in that office at the club, wondering if I'm going to be raped or killed.

"You're an asshole, you know that?" I huff out a breath and stand in order to put some distance between us.

He grabs my arm and I glance down at where we're connected. I raise my eyes to meet his and quirk a brow. He doesn't take the hint and maintains his grip. I try to shake him off, but I'm no match for him.

"Jackson," he says. "My real name is Jackson Stark." He drops my arm and shifts on the couch. "And I'm not an asshole. Not really."

He sounds so much like a petulant child, and something in me snaps. As much as I try to stop myself, I can't contain the very un-ladylike snort that escapes or the laughter that bubbles over.

"What's so funny?" There's genuine confusion in his tone and that only incites more laughter.

My side aches from laughing so hard, and my jaw is screaming at me. I finally manage to calm myself down, and after a few deep breaths, I school my features and face him.

"You're fucking crazy," he accuses. "I don't know why I risked my career to save your ass." He stands and walks around the couch before bracing his hands on the back and shaking his head. "A year of my life, down the drain. And for what? A stripper who had me so tied in knots and second-guessing everything? A woman who made me want things I couldn't have?"

I stare at him, dumbfounded by the words spewing out of his mouth. He's not really talking to me, more like rambling to no one in particular, but I can't stop listening.

"I don't need this. You're the one who made a deal with the devil. You're the one who got yourself in that position. Why should I save you only to ruin myself?" He finally looks up and stares at me, so hard it's like he's looking for my soul. "Huh? Tell me. Why should I help you?"

"Because you're a good man." I slam my mouth shut. I don't know what made me say that. I'm not even real clear on why I think that. All I know is he's had every opportunity to hurt me, to send me packing and salvage what he could of his undercover operation, but he hasn't. He's tended to my wounds, made sure I got clean, and held me when I broke. I may not know him, but I do know he's not the man he's pretending to be for Kevin Vick.

"That's where you're wrong, darlin'." He stalks toward me and thrusts his fingers through my hair and tugs, forcing my head up to look at him. "I'm not a good man."

His lips crash into mine and for a second, my fight or flight response kicks in, and I struggle against him. When he doesn't relent, I let myself get swept up in the kiss. I part my lips, granting his insistent tongue access to what it's seeking. He tastes like whiskey with a dash of desperation. Or maybe the desperation is all mine.

I flatten my hands against his chest and hate the fact that his T-shirt is preventing me from feeling flesh. I slide my fingertips down his sides until I reach the hem of his shirt and lift it up, baring him to my touch. The second my nails bite into him, he tugs my hair harder, pulling my head back and nipping my neck. He uses his free hand to pull the T-shirt off my shoulder and the sound of fabric ripping fuels the flames licking my body.

"I'm not a good man," he growls before lapping at my collarbone like a sexually starved man.

I dig my nails in deeper, not caring that I'll break skin if I don't let up. Moans fill the air around us, and I realize they're coming from me. I want to crawl up this man's body and melt into him.

"Please," I beg, although I'm not quite sure what I'm begging for. Him to ease the ache between my legs or one of us to come to our senses and stop this madness. "Please, Jack."

His assault on my collarbone stops, and his body tenses. When he steps away, I'm left feeling cold, exposed, aching. He thrusts a frustrated hand in his hair.

"Fuck!" he rages. He turns away from me, and his shoulders rise and fall as he takes deep breaths. After several, he turns back around, and the look on his face is heartbreaking. "My name is Jackson. Not Jack. I will never be Jack to you."

"I'm sorry. I didn't mean—"

"Don't worry about it." He tosses the blanket at me. "Cover yourself up before I forget all the reasons I wish I weren't a good man."

I wrap the blanket around my shoulders and curl up into a ball in the corner of the couch. I stare at him, waiting for him to say something, anything, to make me forget that I almost let myself be taken by a complete stranger. When he doesn't speak, I can't take the silence, so I try to fill it.

"Jackson, we should talk."

5

JACKSON

Why is it that when a woman says 'we should talk', every man in the history of forever feels his balls start to shrivel, and a knot of dread forms in the deepest pit of his stomach? And I don't even get the make-up sex after this particular *talk*.

"There's nothing to talk about, Kitty Kat." I see the hurt flash in her eyes at the use of her stage name. I know I'm being a dick, but when she called me Jack, it had been ice water to my overheated body. My desire sizzled and went up in a puff of smoke. I want her to experience what I did in that moment.

I storm out of the room and leave her standing there, mouth gaping open. As much as I want to leave the house entirely, I can't. I'm trapped in this hell of my own making. I slam the bathroom door behind me and flip the lock.

Memories are beginning to assault me, hammer at my soul, making it impossible to focus on my anger at Katelyn. Memories I've tried like hell to bury, memories that tug and pull at me until I follow them into the abyss.

I drop down to the floor and hang my head, letting them

come and hating that there's not a damn thing I can do to stop them.

"Jackson, we need to talk."

Melinda stares at me from the rocking chair. She's feeding Ben, and what should be a beautiful moment is tainted by the scowl on her face.

"Mel, not now."

I step into the nursery and bend to kiss my son's downy head. His little hand reaches toward me, and I let him wrap his fingers around mine. He gets stronger and bigger every day and for a moment, I consider going AWOL so I don't have to miss any of it.

"If not now, then when?" Melinda fiercely whispers. "You deploy tomorrow and who knows when we'll see each other again, let alone get to talk."

A tear slips down her cheek, and I swipe at it with my thumb. I hate seeing her cry, and I despise knowing it's because of me. My wife is the love of my life, and I'm putting so much on her right now. A newborn, caring for her mother after her surgery. And let's not forget doing this all alone because of my fucked up sense of honor.

In my defense, when I joined the military, I hadn't known Melinda. We had a whirlwind romance, and she knew what she was signing up for when she married me. What she hadn't agreed to was me re-upping. She was pregnant and we'd agreed that I'd finish out my last few months and then we'd be a family, but when the time came, I couldn't do it. I wasn't ready to say good-bye to the Army, to my friends, the men who had become a second family to me.

"I'm coming back to you, baby."

I lean over to place a kiss on her cheek, and she turns away. Tears are freely falling from her eyes, and for the first time since I re-upped, I feel real fear. Not because I'm being deployed and could be killed. No. I'm scared because I'm not sure my family will be here waiting for me. And the next words out of her mouth only intensify that fear.

"I hope and pray you come back, alive and in one piece." She returns her gaze to mine and smiles sadly. *"I'm just not sure Benny and I will be here when you do."*

As the memory fades and reality returns, I realize that someone is pounding on the front door and someone is furiously whispering just beyond the bathroom door.

"Jackson! Please Jackson, I'm sorry." It's Katelyn and she sounds terrified. "They're here. I don't know what to do. Jett and Stoner, they're outside and I'm afraid if you don't answer your door they'll break it down."

Her words register, and I shoot up off the floor. I open the bathroom door and drag her inside. She's trembling and her eyes are as wide as saucers. I pull my gun from my waistband, and although it doesn't seem possible, her eyes grow wider.

"You're gonna kill me? Just like that?" Her bottom lip wobbles, and all of her spunk from earlier is gone.

"This isn't for you." I eject the clip and check to see how many rounds are left. Satisfied that there's enough, I pop it back in. I keep the gun in my left hand, and with my right, I wrap my fingers around her neck and pull her in for a quick, hard kiss. "Lock the door behind me. No matter what you hear, you stay here and don't open the door until I tell you."

I don't wait for her to respond, just exit the bathroom, and when I hear the lock click into place behind me, all I can think is *good girl*.

I make my way to the front door, and when I throw it open, I point my weapon right between Stoner's eyes.

"What the fuck, boys?" I snarl.

"Mr. Vick wants to see you," Jett says. I see his lips twitch out of the corner of my eye, but I can't tell if he's laughing at my reaction or at the utter shock on Stoner's face. "Says you're not answering his calls."

I pull my cell phone out of my pocket and glance at the notifications. Ten missed calls from the bastard. Fuck!

"Hard to answer calls that aren't coming in," I lie, tucking my phone back into my pocket. I'm speaking to Jett, but my gaze hasn't wavered from Stoner.

"Get that fuckin' thing outta my face." Stoner pops his knuckles and his muscles flex under his shirt. He thinks he's scaring me, but all he's succeeding in doing is pissing me the fuck off.

"Tell Mr. Vick that I'll be in shortly. As soon as I wrap things up with Kitty Kat." I inject as much disgust into my tone as possible. "Gotta say, she's not quite the purring kitten I was hoping for."

"Is that right?" Stoner sneers. "I can take her off your hands."

"Not necessary." I lower my weapon before I can no longer control my trigger finger. "She is tits and ass after all. She'll get the job done. I'll make sure of that."

"Make it quick. After last night, Mr. Vick's getting twitchy, and I'm not covering for your ass."

Jett starts to turn away, and I grab his arm to stop him, squeezing as hard as I can. Stoner steps toward me, arm drawn back and Jett puts his hand up to stop him. Stoner drops his arm, but he isn't happy about it.

"Are you forgetting who you're talking to? You're my bitch, not the other way around," I remind him. I'm head of security. These two are pawns in a nasty game they don't even realize they're playing.

Jett eyes me up and down before replying. "I'm nobody's bitch."

He yanks out of my hold, and he and Stoner walk down the walkway and get in the waiting black SUV. I stand there, watching, until they pull away from the curb and fly down the street, not bothering to stop at the intersection and narrowly missing another car.

When I'm sure they're gone and not returning, I close the door and throw the deadbolt. I retrace my steps to the bathroom, and just when I'm about to knock and tell Katelyn she can come out, I hear it.

Katelyn's quiet crying drifts through the door, and rather than insist she let me in, I brace my head against the wooden barrier and listen. I have no doubt that this would be a full blown meltdown if she knew that Mr. Vick's enforcers had left and couldn't hear her. I envisioned her, sitting on the floor, knees drawn to her chest and head buried in her hands. When she sniffles, I picture her wiping her nose on the sleeve of my shirt, and for some reason, that doesn't disgust me. It makes me sad.

When I can't stand it any longer, I wrap my knuckles on the door.

"Katelyn, it's me," I say, trying to keep any and all emotion from my voice. "You can open the door."

There's movement and a click when she disengages the lock. She opens the door a crack and peeks out at me. Her eyes are puffy and her nose is red. Jesus, how much crying could a woman do in the span of a few minutes?

"Which you is it?" she asks with a little snark in her tone. She lowers her head and I follow her gaze to the gun still in my hand. "Jack or Jackson?"

I heave a sigh and shove the gun back in my waistband. When my hands are free, I hold them up so she can see that I have nothing to hurt her with.

"Just me... Jackson."

She eyes me warily but must decide to trust me because she opens the door and throws herself at me, wrapping her arms around my waist and holding on like her life depends on it. I'm stunned but then I remember that I don't actually hate this woman and I'm not Jack right now.

I bend to lift her into my arms, and she nestles her head into the crook of my neck. I carry her to the bedroom and lay her down. She hesitates before letting go of my neck, but once she does, she curls into a ball and yawns.

I pull the covers over her body and bend to kiss her cheek before I catch myself and straighten. I shove my hands in my pockets and rock back on my heels. Her eyes have drifted closed, and she hasn't witnessed any of this, thank God. I stare at her a moment longer and debate on crawling in next to her, but quickly dismiss that idea. Resigned to sleeping on the too-short couch, I sigh.

"Get some sleep, Katelyn. We'll talk later."

And because I must be a masochist, I bend and kiss her hair and breathe in her scent before turning on my heel and silently leaving the room.

I'll let her get a few hours of sleep before I figure out how to handle Mr. Vick's twitch.

6

KATELYN

The squeak of the door has me cursing rundown houses. Didn't this guy know how to use WD-40? When there's enough space for me to squeeze through, I step out into the hall and tiptoe my way toward the living room, wincing every time the floorboards creak under my weight.

Jackson is asleep on the couch, and for a moment, I forget that I'm trying to escape. I forget the things I overheard when he was talking to Jett and Stoner just a few hours ago. I forget my deal with the devil and even how to breathe.

He's got one leg dangling over the edge, and the other is sticking over the arm of the sofa. One arm is flung over his eyes, and the other rests on his bare chest. In only boxer briefs and sporting morning wood, even though it's early afternoon, he looks nothing like the man that works for Mr. Vick. He looks almost peaceful and so damn tempting he should be illegal.

I shake my thoughts out of my head and make my way to the door, cursing when the click of the deadbolt fills the silence.

"Leaving so soon?"

I whirl around at Jackson's question. He's sitting up with a smug look on his face. I force a smile and shrug.

"I had to try," I quip and walk to the kitchen. If I'm going to be stuck here, or worse, returned to my hell on Earth, I'm going to need coffee.

I rummage through cupboards until I find what I'm looking for and then start the task of making my daily jolt of make-me-feel-human juice. I hear his footsteps before I see his shadow fall across the counter. His hands rest on my shoulders, and there's no anger in his touch.

"I know," he says, his tone resigned and matter-of-fact. When he breaks contact and steps up next to me, I swallow past the lump in my throat. He's still bare chested, but at least he had the decency to put some pants on. "Katelyn, let's talk."

"You're going to take me back, aren't you?" The question is out before I can stop it. I need to go back, finish out the deal, but for once in my life, I don't want to do the right thing. I want to do the 'me' thing.

He heaves a sigh and wraps his hand around the back of his neck.

"I know you don't believe this, but I don't want to."

The coffee pot beeps to let us know the brew is ready. Jackson grabs two mugs from the cupboard and hands me one. Once we both have our caffeine fix, we sip silently, eyeing each other over the rims. He refills his mug pretty quickly and gives me an odd look before walking toward the living room.

He looks over his shoulder and asks, "You comin'?"

I make my way to the couch and sit on the opposite end as him. I can't help but flash back to the scene I walked in on earlier, and I focus my attention on his face. The sleeping Adonis is gone.

"You said that I signed your death warrant." Pain flashes in his eyes, but he quickly masks it. "Care to elaborate?"

"I told you, protect my family, and I'll give you information." I take a sip of my coffee while I watch the wheels turn in his head.

"You freaked out when I tried to do that. I can't protect them if you don't let me call my partner. I may be FBI, but I'm undercover and can't do it on my own."

I shrug. "Not my problem. I've already resigned myself to what I have to do. You want my help, you find another way."

He gets up and walks to the desk, where he grabs another phone from the same drawer as before. How many phones does one person need? He comes back and when he sits, he stares at the device like he's afraid it's going to turn into a snake and strike. His focus shifts to me, then back to the phone and then back to me again.

"I'm gonna need you to trust me," he says. There's a pleading quality to his voice but there's also something else. Resignation, sadness, fear.

I give a tight nod. What more do I have to lose? If he calls his partner or whatever, I'll just have to find a way to leave.

It takes him a few more minutes of internal debate before he dials a number and puts the phone to his ear. Seeming to think twice, he extends the phone in front of him and puts it on speaker phone. I arch a brow at him, and he lifts a shoulder, lets it fall.

"Who the fuck is this?" a deep voice growls from the other end of the call.

Jackson doesn't say anything, just sits there and stares.

"You've got tw—"

"Micah, it's me," Jackson interrupts and then clears his throat.

"Jackson?"

"I need a favor."

Micah barks out a humorless laugh. "You're fucking kidding me, right? You take off over a year ago, no word to anyone, and now you want a favor? You've got balls, I'll give you that."

I narrow my eyes at Jackson. This guy is his plan? This Micah character is supposed to be my family's lifeline? We're all screwed.

Jackson is rubbing at the creases in his forehead, and his mouth opens and closes several times, no words coming out.

"Nothing to say?" Micah snarls. "The Brotherhood has been nothing but good to you, but you did us dirty. Do you have any idea the shitstorm we were in with Scarlett after you left?"

Unable to stand the verbal lashing directed at Jackson, I speak up.

"Look, I don't know who you are, but he's calling for me." There's steel in my tone and even as I'm grateful for it, I'm praying it doesn't bite me in the ass.

"Micah, I can explain." Jackson finally speaks up. "I promise, I'll explain but first, I need your help with protection for a family."

"It's for my family," I interject.

Jackson glares at me, but I don't care. He clearly doesn't have the relationship with Micah that he thinks he does. And it's *my* family that's at stake here.

"My name is Katelyn Dawson." I swallow and lower my eyes, avoiding Jackson's stare. "I'm a stripper at The White Lily. I don't know what the Brotherhood is or who Scarlett is, but I do know that, right now, Jackson is my only hope of getting my life, my *real* life, back. And apparently I'm his last ditch effort to bring down Kevin Vick. But I can't help if I know my family isn't safe."

"Kevin Vick?" Disgust drips from Micah's tone. "Jackson, is what she's saying true? You're trying to take down that fucker?"

"You know him?" Jackson demands.

Micah heaves a sigh. "We know *of* him. We've had a few of his girls here over the years. He's a crafty motherfucker. Never could link the girls to him other than with their word. And you know as well as I do, the word of strippers isn't always taken as gospel. No offense, ma'am."

"We had an understanding!" Jackson shouts. "You were supposed to bring your cases to me, keep me in the loop so I could do things the right way."

"Keep telling yourself that if it helps you sleep at night. We did what we had to, which is more than I can say for you those last days."

"As much fun as it is to listen to you verbally compare dick sizes, can we focus? Please?" They're acting like children, and we'll get nowhere if they keep it up.

"Jackson, this isn't over."

"Didn't think it would be." Jackson's grip on the phone is so tight it looks like he's lost all circulation. His fingers are white, and his hand is shaking. "Are you gonna help or not?"

"Of course, we'll help. We're pissed, not monsters."

"Jesus, was that so hard? Why couldn't you have just said 'yes' in the first place?"

"What fun would that have been?"

Both men start chuckling, and I'm left reeling, my head spinning in confusion. Over the next few minutes, Jackson has me relay information about my family to Micah. Every once in a while, Micah interjects with a grunt or a question, but other than that, he's quiet as he gets all the details.

The call ends with Micah promising to have 'his best guys, Griffin and Aiden' start their protection detail within the hour. I don't want my family to know they're being watched, or to be told about my less than stellar life choices, which is why I freaked out when Jackson tried to call his partner. Surely the FBI would have to give them some kind of information. I could be wrong but I'm not willing to take that chance. I explain all of this to Micah and Jackson and make Micah promise that his guys will be discreet. He does and Jackson promises him to call in a day or two for that explanation Micah wants.

Jackson disconnects the call and grins from ear to ear. I don't know what he's smiling about. Don't get me wrong, I'm happy he got Micah to agree to help, but I have no idea who these people are. I could have just sent Satan himself to watch over my family.

That's what you get for keeping secrets.

"You can trust them. The Broken Rebel Brotherhood are good people."

I nod. I don't have a choice. I have to believe what he's telling me.

"Now, I did what you asked. I got protection for your parents and brother." He picks his coffee mug up from the table, takes a sip. "It's your turn to start talking."

I get up and start to pace. I don't want to tell him my story. He thinks he knows me, everything about me, but what he doesn't know will prove how naive I was, how stupid I was, and how unworthy of his protection I am.

"Whatever it is, it's not as bad as you think." He steps in front of me, blocking me from continuing to wear a worn path in the hardwood. "Just start from the beginning."

Resigned to the fact that I don't have a choice, I start talking. Details spill out of me at a rapid rate.

"I had a normal childhood, for the most part. Good parents, a younger brother who idolized me." I look past him, stare at the wall. I can feel his eyes bore into my skin, but I resist the urge to focus on him. "I graduated high school with honors, went to college and graduated summa cum laude. Shit didn't start to hit the fan until I tried to find a job. It's not easy to find a teaching position that actually pays enough to cover the bills, and while my parents offered to help me, I wanted to do it on my own, ya know?"

"I get it. Believe me, I do. But how do you go from that to making a deal with Kevin Vick?"

I laugh, humorlessly. "I couldn't find a job. Student loans were kicking in. My best friend from high school, Brandie, told me about a job opportunity that would allow me to make enough money to make those student loan payments every month and still have plenty left over." I finally glance at him. My eyes burn with unshed tears, but I refuse to let them fall. "Brandie was the fun one, the adventurous one. If she wasn't finding trouble, it was finding her. It was never anything serious but even if it were, I didn't care. I was desperate and figured she'd never done anything to put me at risk before, so why would she now, ya know?"

"She introduced you to Vick." It's more a statement than a question.

"She did. I didn't like it, but after talking to him and hearing his assurances that nothing bad would happen, I agreed to try it. One night and if I didn't like it, I'd walk away, no questions asked. Mr. Vick agreed."

"Bastard," he sneers, and then his face scrunches up, as if he's trying to search for some hidden detail in his brain. "How come I don't know anyone at the club named Brandie?"

"She didn't work at The White Lily. I didn't know that at first." I wave my hand like it's no big deal. No big thing that I didn't see the signs, the red flags. "Anyway, I hated my first night. The customers were repulsive and definitely not the 'hard working men' that just 'wanted to blow off some steam' Mr. Vick portrayed. I knew within the first ten minutes that I wasn't going to be safe, that my bills weren't important enough to put up with that kind of bullshit." I shrug. "So I went to Mr. Vick, thinking he'd honor our agreement. I don't like it, I can leave."

"I remember that night, your first night," he says with a smile. "I could tell you were scared, not used to the life. I wanted to haul you off the stage and shelter you from it, but I couldn't risk my cover."

"It's not your fault, Jackson, so forget about it. I'm a big girl. I can take care of myself."

"Right." I want to smack the sarcasm out of him but refrain.

"Do you wanna hear the rest or not?"

"Yeah, sorry." He motions for me to continue.

"I went to him, told him I was sorry but I didn't think stripping was for me. He went from accommodating potential boss to crazy psycho in one second flat. Completely flipped out and said I wasn't leaving, that I'd made him more money my first night than any other girl ever has. That with practice and more experience, I'd continue to make him a 'very rich man.'" I shiver, remembering the terror that had washed over me that night. "He started pulling out pictures from a file on his desk. Pictures of my parents sitting at a restaurant, pictures of my brother walking on his college campus. I was horrified. He said if I didn't continue to work for him, they would suffer."

Jackson traces a finger down my cheek and then grips my chin, forcing my eyes to meet his. "That shouldn't have happened." His face is twisted with rage, but his voice and his touch are calm, gentle. "I will never let him hurt you. Not again."

"Don't make promises you can't keep," I whisper. Hurt flashes across his face, but it's gone so quickly that I think I'm seeing things. "He made a deal with me that night. I give him one year, with a set amount due each month, and not only will he ensure my student loans are paid but my family will be left alone. I agreed. I didn't see any other choice." All of a sudden, it's too much. The memories, the shame, the embarrassment. I quit holding back the tears and let them fall. "I learned real quick how to shut my mind off when I'm on the stage. Pretend I'm somewhere else, someone else."

"You're a natural up there. After that first time, I figured you just got over your nerves. But there was always something in the back of my mind screaming at me that you didn't belong. So I dug into you, made it my mission to learn everything I possibly could about you." He sits down on the edge of the coffee table and braces his elbows on his knees. "Where does Brandie factor into all this? You said she got you the job but that she doesn't work at the club."

"She did and she doesn't." My throat feels like it's going to close up, the emotion so thick I can't suck in air past it. "You know that The White Lily is just a cover, right?"

He nods. "For a drug ring, yeah."

"Yeah, there's that. But that doesn't even begin to cover what he's doing." I tilt my head and stare at him. He really has no idea. "As his head of security, I figured you'd know all about his business. Every dirty detail."

"Apparently not." He shakes his head with disdain. "What don't I know?"

"Brandie was part of the escort service."

"Fuck!" he roars and jumps up to pace. He stops and his body stiffens before he focuses his intense eyes on me. "Wait. You said 'was'."

"She was. Until she was sold to pay off one of Mr. Vick's debts. I don't know where she is now, haven't seen or heard from her for a month."

7

JACKSON

Human trafficking? Sex trafficking? One time deal?

The possibilities are endless, and my mind is racing. None of this should surprise me though. It makes sense. But how did I miss this? How did I not see what was going down right under my nose?

I stare at Katelyn, who's openly crying now, and my heart bleeds for what she's gone through, what she knows. She's young, beautiful, smart. She should never know what evil is, and in that moment, I vow, if only to myself, to make sure that she only knows good from now on.

I move to the couch, next to Katelyn, and pull her onto my lap. She doesn't resist and instead buries her head in the crook of my neck. It's not lost on me how perfectly she fits. I whisper reassurances, stroke her back, while inside the rage is threatening to eat me alive.

By the time she calms down, a vision has emerged. A fantasy really. One that involves killing Kevin Vick with my bare fucking hands, consequences be damned. I won't follow through with it, but it quiets the noise in my head to think about his lifeless body, blood no longer pumping because I stopped his heart.

"I'm sorry," Katelyn murmurs as she wipes her nose on her shoulder and shifts in my lap.

The motion causes my dick to stir and I know she feels it when her eyes lock onto mine. The whites around her irises are bloodshot, her face is bruised, and her nose is red from crying, but she's still the most beautiful woman I've ever seen. I wait for the pain to come at the thought of Melinda, the overwhelming feeling that I'm betraying her, but it doesn't surface.

Katelyn shifts again, this time to straddle me. I know I should stop her, put an end to this madness, but I can't. I won't. If this is what she needs to feel better, I'll give it to her. I'll give her anything she asks for.

I rest my hand against her cheek and brush my thumb across her bottom lip, being careful of the cut. Her pink tongue darts out, tentatively at first. When I groan at the wet contact, she parts her lips further and nips at my thumb before sucking it into her mouth and swirling her tongue around it. Her eyes slide closed and she hums, the vibration traveling to my cock and making my pants feel way too small.

I'm about to come, like some randy teenager who's never experienced the wet heat of a woman before. I pull my hand away, and Katelyn's eyes fly open as she whimpers.

As much as I love the way she looks in my clothes, I need her out of them. I yank the shirt over her head and urge her to stand. When she does, I slide the sweats over her hips, down her thighs, until they pool at her feet. My mouth goes dry at the sight of perfection before me.

Katelyn tries to cover herself, but I grab her wrists to stop her.

"Don't," I beg. "Don't hide from me."

She slowly lowers her arms to her sides. I let my gaze travel from her gorgeous eyes to her pink lips and then lower to her perfectly rounded tits and even lower to the juncture between her thighs. Everywhere my eyes go, goosebumps break out across her flesh. Her skin heats up under my scrutiny and turns a shade of red that tells me she's embarrassed.

She may strip for men on a regular basis, but that's business. This is pleasure.

"Jackson, please," she purrs.

"Please what, darlin'?"

I trace a path from just under her chin to her breasts and circle her nipples, loving how they harden for me, how she shivers beneath my fingertips.

"Make me feel."

"Oh, I'm going to make you feel. You're gonna feel my cock and what you do to it. You're gonna feel how perfectly I know we'll fit. You're gonna feel wet and hot and bothered and *full*. Don't you worry, you're gonna fucking feel."

I surge up from the couch and yank my shirt off over my head. The air against my heated skin is cool but not nearly cool enough to slow me down. I bend and pull a pebbled nipple into my mouth, sucking on it until she's moaning, her head thrown back in a brilliant display of ecstasy.

Her hands grip the waistband of my pants, tugging and pulling, doing anything she can to get them off. I kick them from my feet and lift her up. Her legs wrap around my waist, and I feel her ankles lock at the small of my back as they fuse our bodies even closer together.

Our lips collide in a fiery kiss, passion fueling our actions, desperation pulsing between us. I knead the globes of her ass as I carry her back to the bedroom, never breaking contact with her mouth, and kick the door shut behind me.

I toss her on the bed, and her ankles remain in place so I go down with her. I manage to catch my weight on outstretched arms and slowly lower my body to hers. I reach between us and dip a finger between her folds, teasing her opening. I coat my digit in her juices and drag it up to her clit. The instant I make contact, her hips buck and she cries out.

I continue to torture the bundle of nerves as I lean down and whisper in her ear. "How's that for feeling?"

"M-more. I n-need more."

Katelyn is panting and her nails are digging into my pecs. Not wanting to deny her anything, I glide a finger into her pussy and quickly add a second one while maintaining pressure on her clit with my thumb. I listen to the sounds she makes, the way her body moves to seek release, and when her walls start to clamp down on my fingers, I yank them out and replace them with my cock, slamming into her so hard she surges up on the bed.

Her orgasm milks me, and her cum coats my dick. We're both sweating and I know my own release is close, too close. I pull out and flip her over, wrapping my arm around her waist to pull her up on all fours. Once I'm sure she's steady, I fist my dick and slide it up and down her slit, pumping up and down on it while I taunt her.

When I'm perfectly aligned with her opening, she glances over her shoulder, grins, and then impales herself on me, taking me all the way to the hilt. We both freeze for a moment, me in shock and her I imagine to adjust to this new depth.

I bend over and rain kisses over her spine, nipping here and there until I get to the top of her ass. When I do, I reach up and grab a handful of hair, tugging on it just enough that I know it stings.

"Fuck me, Jackson," she demands in a breathless shout.

"Do you feel what you do to me, how perfect we fit?" I growl as I grip her hip and thrust in and out of her.

She tries to nod but can't with my hand still wrapped around her hair. "Yes."

"Do you feel hot and bothered?"

"Y-yes."

She's matching my thrusts, and the sound of our sweaty flesh slapping as I piston in and out of her echoes in the otherwise still room.

"Are you fucking full, Katelyn? Do I fill you up?"

"So fu… oh God… f-full!"

Her response is punctuated by her walls spasming and her body twitching. I let go of her hair and hold her up as I continue to assail her pussy. Just when I think my legs are about to give out, my balls draw tight and I stiffen, my cock pulsing in her slick, wet heat.

When neither of us have anything else left to give, we collapse in a sweaty heap on the bed. I roll to the side and tug her with me. She tucks herself into my body, her back to my front, and I wrap my arms around her, holding on as if my life depended on it.

"You certainly know how to make a girl feel." There's a sleepy smile in her voice.

I kiss the back of her head, and a smile of my own spreads across my face.

"Jackson?" She tries to hide her yawn but is unsuccessful.

"Hmm?"

"Thank you."

"You don't need to thank me." I huff out a laugh. "It was my pleasure."

She yawns again and this time she makes no effort to contain it.

"Jackson?"

"Yeah, darlin'?"

"You have to take me back, don't you?"

"Shh. Close your eyes. Let me worry about that."

She's right. I have to take her back. But I want to be selfish and irresponsible for a little while longer. I'll make it right with Mr. Vick and make sure it's not taken out on her.

"Jackson?"

"Yeah?"

"I'm gonna help you bring that bastard to his knees." Another yawn. "I trust you to protect me."

8

MR. VICK

"What the fuck do you mean, he's not coming?"

Glass shatters as my tumbler hits the wall. My face is hot, my hands are trembling with rage, and Jett and Stoner are standing in front of me, arms crossed over their chests, flat expressions on their faces.

"Sir, we told him you wanted him to come in. He refused and said he'd be here when he could." Stoner shifts from one foot to the other. At least he seems to have a little fear of me.

Jett, on the other hand, gives away nothing. He's cool as a cucumber and it's pissing me off. I remind myself that I hired him because of his ability to separate himself from the more *unsavory* aspects of the job. The thought is little comfort at the moment.

"Please tell me you at least saw the girl?"

Stoner lowers his gaze to the floor. And there's my answer. I storm across the room and grab him by the lapels of his jacket. I'd like to think I could lift him up and leave his feet dangling, his body quaking in terror, but the man is a beast and doesn't budge. That only serves to fuel my anger.

"You had one fucking job! One! Not only did you not get that done, but you didn't even make sure he had the girl."

I loosen my grip and shove him away from me. Again, he doesn't budge. Dumb motherfucker.

"With all due respect, sir," Jett speaks up. "Mr. Duffy had a gun trained on Stoner the entire time."

"What's your point?" I turn my attention to Jett.

"Well, sir, he would have killed Stoner if we pushed too hard."

"I repeat, what's your point?" If these two think that they can't be replaced, they are useless to me. A scared employee is an obedient employee.

"No point, sir," Jett replies.

"That's what I thought."

I return to my desk and sink into the leather chair. Now what the fuck am I supposed to do? I need Kitty Kat. She didn't know it, but she's the key to fixing all of my problems. Saul Luciano is very satisfied with Brandie, too satisfied. Now he's demanding more. He'd given me his word that Brandie cancelled out my debt, but apparently his word isn't as good as mine. I might be a criminal, but I stick to my word. Mostly.

"Do you want us to go back?" Jett asks, startling me from my thoughts.

Do I? I could order them to return, kill Jack and bring Kitty Kat to me. They'd do it. But then I'd have to go through the process of covering up a murder and looking for a new head of security. Quite frankly, I just don't feel like it. Too much work.

"That won't be necessary, Jett," I finally reply.

I pull out a black ledger from my top drawer, as well as the baggie from the hidden compartment at the back. I toss both on my desk. I find what I'm looking for in the ledger and scribble down the details for their next assignment. I thrust the little piece of scrap paper at Stoner. Sure, I could text the details, but paper is safer. Paper can be burned. Texts can be traced.

Stoner takes the note and reads it, his eyebrows raising. He hands it to Jett when he's done, and Jett's reaction to the words is swifter, harsher.

"Sir, isn't this a little harsh? I mean, isn't it too soon for this?"

Like a good soldier, Stoner snatches the paper from Jett's fingertips and pulls a lighter from his pocket. When the paper ignites, Stoner drops it into the metal trash can next to the desk and watches it burn. It doesn't take long and just like that, no evidence.

"Maybe, but it's all we've got. Is this going to be a problem?" I brace my elbows on the desk and fold my hands, choosing my next words carefully. "Jett, if this is going to be a problem, Stoner can handle it on his own and when he's done, I'm sure you can imagine what his next task will be." I raise one eyebrow at him, daring him to challenge me further.

"No problem, sir."

Jett turns and walks out of the office. Something about his reaction seems off. He's been working for me for almost two years and has never questioned my orders. Not really. He's given some good reasons why certain things might not work, but all of his advice is more tactical in nature, not moral. I'll have to keep an eye on that one.

Stoner follows him, and just before he can step through the door, I call out and he turns around.

"Keep him in line," I bark.

A grin tugs at the corners of his mouth, and a chill races down my spine at the crazy I see. Stoner has always had a screw loose, and I just hope and pray that he never unleashes his madness on me.

"Yes, sir."

When they're both gone, I review my options if they can't get this assignment done. I have none, unless I want to get my hands dirty. I don't. I pay them well so I don't have to, and it's been the right move so far. I've been arrested more times than I can count. As recently as last night, in fact. But because I have staff, my lawyer is always able to get me out quickly. This time, I'd been out in under four hours, a record.

I pick up the baggie I'd retrieved a few minutes ago and stare at it. When I first got into the drug business, I'd never before touched the stuff. Then I'd started testing the product here and there, making sure my buyers got what they paid for. That morphed into occasionally getting high with a few trusted people, sort of like social drinking. I snort at the thought.

I dump the contents out of the plastic baggie, not bothering to protect the surface of my desk. I scrape the white powder into a perfect line with a piece of paper. When I'm satisfied that it's exactly right, I push against one side of my nose and bend, snorting the cocaine up the other side. I throw my head back and blow out a breath.

Now, I wait.

9

KATELYN

"You can just throw the clothes on the floor. I'll pick them up later."

Jackson let me sleep for an hour or two, but my respite is over. When he woke me up, he said that it was time to go back to The White Lily. I didn't want to, but I told him I would help and I meant the rest of what I said, too. I trusted him to keep me safe.

"Got it," I mumble, standing in the bathroom doorway and staring at my feet.

Jackson grips my chin and forces me to look at him.

"Katelyn, nothing is going to happen to you. I promise."

"I kn—"

"Hold that thought," Jackson says when his cell phone pings with an incoming text.

His eyes narrow and his face turns an alarming shade of red.

"Fuck," he roars.

He thrusts the fingers of his free hand through his hair before he whirls around and punches the wall, his fist leaving a hole and his knuckles coming away bloody. I flinch at his sudden outburst but other than that, don't move.

"Jackson?"

"Go get changed, now," he demands. He starts scrolling through his phone, uncaring about the red ooze coating the screen as he does, and when I don't move, he nudges me through the door and pulls it shut.

Left alone with no other choice than to do what he says, I quickly strip my borrowed clothes from my body. I hold his shirt to my nose and inhale his scent before dropping it to the floor. I catch sight of myself in the mirror and wince. My eye isn't as swollen, thanks to the iBuprofen and ice Jackson gave me, but it's a shade of purple and blue that's alarming. The cut on my lip is starting to scab over, and for that, I'm grateful.

I don't know how Mr. Vick expects me to earn him much money with the wounds he's inflicted visible, but maybe I can cover them with makeup. At least enough so that they aren't as noticeable through the haze of smoke in the club.

I yank my clothes from the shower curtain rod, where I'd left them after Jackson had forced me to shower. They were dry, thank God. At least I wouldn't have to return to the club a wet mess. I shimmy into the spandex and mesh garments, feeling way too exposed. When I'm dressed, I go to open the door, but stop myself. I don't want Jackson to see me like this. He's seen me naked, but somehow, this feels different. This feels... cheap.

I scoop up his discarded T-shirt and pull it over my head, covering myself. Satisfied that I've maintained a little modesty, I exit the bathroom and follow the sound of his voice to the kitchen. He doesn't hear me enter, and his back is to the room as he stares out the window over the sink.

"I don't give a damn what you have to do, make it right."

I have no idea who he's talking to and I'm not sure I want to know. I listen as he continues.

"No, I haven't told her." He huffs out a laugh, and alarm bells blare in my head. "I need her to trust me. That's the only way to get this done."

My heart sinks. I do trust him. Or I had before this phone call. I start to turn away from him, to flee, and the floor creaks under my weight. Jackson whirls around at the sound, and his expression is that of a man who just got caught cheating.

"Shit! Gotta go." He ends the call before tossing it on the table. "Katelyn, it's not what you think."

Unable to control my temper, I stalk to him and stab a finger at his chest. "You have no clue what I think!"

I twist to storm away but only manage to make it one step. He wraps his arms around my waist, holding me in place. He pulls me closer and when I struggle against his hold, he tightens his grip and rests his chin on my head.

"This doesn't change anything," I pout, folding my arms over my chest.

"And neither did my phone call." He sighs and urges me to face him. When I do, his face softens. "I promised to keep you safe and I will. I like you, Katelyn. More than I have a right to, given the circumstances and my—" He slams his mouth shut and shakes his head. "Nevermind. It doesn't matter."

He drops his arms and steps back, shoving his hands in his pockets. He looks so dejected, and my instinct is to reach out and comfort him but first, I need some answers.

"Jackson, talk to me," I plead. "You expect me to trust you, but that goes both ways." I take a tentative step toward him, stand with only inches separating us. "You know so much about me and I know nothing about you other than your name and your profession. Talk to me. Please."

"I can't," he pushes out. He straightens and squares his shoulders. "We should go."

He stalks out of the kitchen, swiping his cell off the table as he passes it. It takes me several seconds to get my feet to move and follow.

What the hell just happened?

He wants me to believe that nothing has changed when in reality, everything has. My life as I knew it is over. That should make me happy. That would make most women in my position happy. But all it does for me is bring a sense of dread.

Last night, I'd been a girl who knew what was expected of her and had a vague idea of what to expect of others. Sure, it was never anything good, but I'd accepted that.

Now, I had no idea what to expect. Will Jackson keep his word or will he succumb to his role as Jack Duffy?

∼

The drive back to The White Lily is silent. Jackson drives with a careless ease that should make me feel better, but the scowl on his face betrays the calm he's projecting. When he pulls into the parking lot, he points to the glove box.

"Open that for me."

I push the button and let the door to the compartment drop open. In it are two things: a gun and a cell phone. I make no move to grab either.

"I need you to take that phone," Jackson's gaze shifts to me before returning back to the parking lot in front of him. "It's a burner, so it can't be traced. If you need to get in touch with me for any reason, use it. I'm going to do my best to stay as close to you as possible, but if this doesn't go my way, I want you prepared."

"I have my own phone. Besides, won't you need it?"

"Like I said, your phone can be traced. And you don't need to worry about me, darlin." He winks as he throws the SUV in park and cuts the engine. "I've got plenty of burner phones."

I take the cell and stare at it in my lap. I have no where to put it. Jackson had whisked me away from this place before I could grab my stuff out of my locker, and it's not like I have pockets. He seems to realize my predicament and swears under his breath before grabbing the phone and shoving it in his pocket.

"I'll make sure it gets to your locker." He reaches across me to grab the gun that remains in the glove box.

"I'm not touching th—"

"This is for me." He checks for bullets and when he finds the clip full, he sticks the gun at the small of his back. "I'll have to teach you how to shoot, but for now, stick to using those stilettos of yours and anything else handy if you need a weapon."

"Jesus," I mumble. "Please tell me you have a plan. Some way to ensure I don't ever have to be alone."

Jackson's eyes search mine as if he's debating what he can and can't tell me. Apparently satisfied with what he sees, he says, "I do but you're just going to have to trust me."

"Why won't you tell me?"

"The less you know, the better. Trust me."

"You keep saying I need to trust you, but I gotta say, that's not so easy after that phone call. You're keeping secrets and I don't like it."

"It's for your own good."

When I give him a frustrated glare, he heaves a sigh.

"After work, I'll fill you in, okay?" He cups my cheek and I lean into him. "For now, my promise to keep you safe, no matter what happens, has to be enough."

I savor his touch a moment longer before nodding. I take

a deep breath and turn away to push open the door and step out into the cool air. The parking area is empty other than a few staff vehicles and the ominous black sedan that Mr. Vick insists he be chauffeured around in.

Jackson's car door slams, and I jump at the sound. My breathing becomes shallow, and black dots dance in front of my face. Images of being handcuffed to the chair in Mr. Vick's office swirl in my head, and my knees threaten to give out.

"Darlin', breathe." Jackson's hands on my shoulders pull me back into reality, and I suck in air. "Good girl. Now, we're gonna go in there and you're going to follow my lead, okay?"

I give a tight nod and continue to breathe as deeply as I can.

"Just remember, within those four walls," he points to the building over his shoulder and continues, "I'm Jack Duffy. I'm playing a role, nothing more."

"O-okay," I stammer.

He grips the hem of my T-shirt and yanks it off over my head. I shiver and fold my arms to cover myself. He gives me an apologetic look.

"Sorry, but you've got a role to maintain, too. I need Kitty Kat to come out and play."

I hear his words, but they take a minute to register. Once they do, I square my shoulders and move to walk past him. I hear his chuckle behind me and a mumbled 'that's my girl' and that only fuels my need to get this right.

For me.

For my family.

For *him.*

10

JACKSON

"Nice of you to finally show up, Jack."

Mr. Vick is standing behind his desk, and while his words are directed at me, he's leering at Katelyn. My blood boils, threatening to sear my veins, but I don't let that show. Katelyn and I both have roles to play, and if we don't, there's no telling what will happen. I do, however, narrow my eyes at him so he knows that I'm not some limp dick flunkie he can walk all over.

"I was enjoying my reward." I tilt my head to indicate Katelyn, who's standing next to me with her back straight and showing no sign of the fear or hatred I know she's feeling.

"Is that right? I was told that she wasn't getting the job done."

"Kitty Kat got the job done," I say as I swat Katelyn's ass, the crack of my palm on her barely covered flesh stinging a bit. "Just took a little longer than I'd hoped."

"And you Kitty Kat? Did Jack get the job done for you?" Mr. Vick steps around his desk and sidles up to Katelyn's back, his mouth close to her ear. I see her roll her eyes as she nods, and I fight to keep my laugh in. "I can't hear you!" he yells as he grabs a fistful of hair and yanks her head back.

"Y-yes."

He shoves her head forward, letting go of her hair. Mr. Vick circles Katelyn, and as he does, he traces a fingertip over her flesh. When I can't take it anymore, this vile man touching my woman, I grab his arm and twist it behind his back, enjoying his roar of pain.

"Let go," he snarls.

I do, realizing that I potentially just blew my plan all to hell. *Fuck!* Mr. Vick cradles his arm against his body and for a second, he looks like he's going to tear into me. He surprises me though and starts to laugh. He returns to his spot behind his desk and stands there, his gaze darting back and forth between Katelyn and me.

"I'm gonna chalk that up to all of the blood in your body being rerouted to your dick," he says to me. "But make no mistake, if it happens again, you'll not only be out of a job, you're life as you know it will be over."

"It won't happen again." I take a deep breath before saying the words that could jeopardize everything. "On one condition."

Mr. Vick bristles and quirks a brow. He's not used to people giving him conditions, but it's all I've got right now and it worked before. He sits down and tips his office chair back like he doesn't have a care in the world. He does. We all do.

"And what's that?" he asks.

"I want Kitty Kat all to myself." I watch him, trying to determine what he's thinking as I speak. I can't figure him out so I continue. "It may have taken a bit for her to warm up, but she's exactly what I crave, for my *kinks*. I don't give a damn if she bares all on stage, but her pussy belongs to me."

Mr. Vick looks at me with suspicious, cold eyes. He's

giving away nothing, and I ignore the urge to swallow past the lump in my throat. After several tense minutes, he throws his head back and laughs.

"Jack, Jack, Jack. What took you so long?" He leans forward and braces his elbows on his oak desk.

"Sir?" That is not the reaction I was expecting.

"Jack, I've watched you for a while now. You've taken home a few of the waitresses, availed yourself of a few of the club extras, but other than that, you're pretty much a lone wolf. Keep to yourself, keep your head down, do your job. I admire that in my head of security." He pauses and eyes Katelyn. "All of the other men have asked for extra pussy to be sent their way, but not you."

"I don't dip my dick just anywhere," I snap, frustrated with the way he talks about the women he employs like they're nothing more than a piece of meat, a product.

"You're a better man than most," he chuckles.

"He's not a good man," Katelyn speaks up and then quickly ducks her head.

I whirl on her and wrap my hand around her throat. I don't exert any pressure but you'd never know it by the expression on her face.

"You'll speak when spoken to, Kitty Kat," I growl. "Or have you already forgotten my rules?" She stares at me, wide eyed and silent. "Answer me!"

"I'm sorry," she pushes out.

"I'm sorry..."

"I'm sorry, Master." Her eyes drop to the floor, and at that moment, I want to pull her close and praise her for her performance.

For a second, I almost wish I was into BDSM because she would make an exquisite submissive. Then the second passes, and I remind myself that she's playing a role, just like I am. She's got too much spirit and fight in her to be a sub, and I could never dominate her, not really. I want an equal, and that's exactly what she is.

Getting a little ahead of yourself, don't ya think?

"Here's the thing, Jack," Mr. Vick says from behind steepled hands. "You're little display of, well, whatever the fuck this was, puts me in a bit of a bind."

I release Katelyn's neck and face off with my boss. Katelyn makes a show of sucking in air and holding her throat where there would've been marks had I really meant to hurt her.

"And why's that?" I ask.

Mr. Vick heaves a sigh and stands. "Can I trust you, Jack?"

His question throws me off guard. It's not at all what I expected, and warning bells go off in my head. Is he finally going to give me information I can use? I have to play this right or I could screw the case and Katelyn.

"If you question my loyalty, what the fuck do you keep me around for?"

"Fair point." Mr. Vick walks toward the wall and lifts a painting off its hook, revealing a safe. He glances over his shoulder at me and then returns his attention to punching in a code and opening the steel door. "Here."

He tosses a notebook at me, and I catch it to my chest before opening it and scrolling through its contents. At first glance it appears to be a record of his escort business, but as I read further down the page, my heart drops. This is a book detailing debts Mr. Vick has accumulated and how he's paid them off… with women. It confirms what I suspected based on the information Katelyn already told me: Kevin Vick has his hands in human trafficking, even if it is born out of some sort of twisted way to pay people back. I catch sight of Brandie's name, written halfway down the page, and have to force myself not to react. It's next to a column marked 'debt owed' and there's a black checkmark next to it with the words 'paid in full'.

I glance up from the notebook and pin Mr. Vick with my stare. "What is this?"

"The holy fucking grail, son."

He isn't wrong about that. This is exactly what I need to put him away for life, longer if it were possible.

Mr. Vick turns his attention to Katelyn and he sneers.

"Kitty Kat, go get ready." He glances at his watch. "You're on in a few hours, and I need you looking better than... that." He sweeps his hand to indicate her body as he eyes her from head to toe.

When she turns to leave, I grip her arm and spin her around to face me. She slams into my chest, and I make a show of groping her, pulling her hair, kissing her roughly. She's stiff, at first, and when she melts into the kiss, I know I went too far. Neither of us can control ourselves for long, apparently.

I shove her away and toward the door, smacking her loudly on the ass.

"You really have laid claim to her, haven't you?" Mr. Vick asks, although he seems more amused than anything else.

I shrug. "Tits and ass, boss." I look over my shoulder at the empty doorway. "Incredible fucking pussy, too."

"I like you, Jack. I really do. Which is why I'm going to give you a chance to earn Kitty Kat."

"Earn her?"

"As you can see," he nods toward the book still in my hand. "I have some debts that I owe. Nothing major," he rushes to add. "But debts, nonetheless. Kitty Kat has debts of her own. I plan to kill two birds with one stone."

"How exactly are you going to do that, sir?" Calling him 'sir' never sat right with me, and it feels even worse now, but I still have a cover to maintain.

"You see, Kitty Kat is here to pay off a debt of her own. Now I'm going to use her to pay off one of mine. Both debts will be cleared and we can all walk away happy."

No, he could walk away happy. Katelyn wouldn't walk away at all. The thought of another man touching her, especially one sleazy enough to be tangled up with Kevin Vick, has me seeing red. I take a step forward, intent on shutting him up for good, but catch myself. He doesn't miss my outrage though.

"Now, now, Jack. It's business. Nothing more. But..." He pauses, making a show of his hesitation. He knows exactly what he wants to say so his display pisses me off.

"Spit it out," I snap before I can stop myself.

"But," he continues. "If you can figure out another way to get my debt to Saul Luciano cleared, Kitty Kat's all yours."

Perfect. I can make that happen. But in the meantime...

"What about while I'm trying to get this done?"

"What about it?" he asks as he tilts his head.

"Kitty Kat's mine," I growl. "If I can't sort this out, I'll give her up, but at least let me play with her while I'm doing your dirty work."

Mr. Vick's eyes narrow, but he doesn't call me out on my 'dirty work' comment. He wouldn't. No, if he's pissed, he'll get someone else to handle it.

"Fine," he finally responds. "But, Jack, I need her in one piece. Luciano doesn't mess around and neither do I."

Relief overwhelms me. I did it. I got him to agree to my plan. Okay, a variation of my plan, but it's something. And something is better than nothing. I can keep an eye on Katelyn, and no one will dare fuck with her if they think she's mine.

"I won't break her." I shrug. "But you don't pay me to be gentle."

"Touche."

11

KATELYN

"Here, kitty kitty."

I roll my eyes at the way Sapphire calls out to me. She finished her set and came walking in the dressing room counting her dollar bills, like she always does. She's a bitch and she flaunts it. She has thick thighs and an ass you could bounce a quarter off of. She's got the body, but her face is lacking, although you'd never know it by the amount of money she brings in.

Not as much as you.

"Saph, when are you gonna quit with that shit?" I ask. "You know I hate it."

"Which is why I keep doing it," she replies, cackling to punctuate her words.

I learned quickly that I had to make nice with the other girls or I'd never survive being a stripper. Not only were the customers repulsive, but the strippers were territorial and bitchy. There isn't one in the bunch who is okay with the fact that I make the most money and never step foot in a VIP booth.

Sapphire steps up behind me and glances at my reflection in the mirror. She fluffs my hair and shakes her head.

"That makeup doesn't hide everything, but it'll have to do."

I drop my head, not trusting myself to not blurt out the truth about how I received the wounds. As it stands, she thinks I have a new boyfriend who got drunk and was a little rough. As if that makes it okay.

My song starts and I stand up, smoothing my hands down tonight's costume: jet black wig, black leather corset with the laces in the front, a leather thong, and stiletto heeled boots that come to mid thigh. As I make my way on stage, I try to find Jackson through the awful lighting and haze of smoke. I don't spot him, and awful scenarios dance in my mind. What if Mr. Vick didn't agree to his plan? What if he pissed Mr. Vick off? What if, what if, what if?

The first song fades and the second starts, and that's when I see him. He's standing by the side door with his arms crossed over his chest and a scowl on his face. I lock eyes with him, and the rest of the club melts away. I'm dancing for him and suddenly want to make this the best I've got.

I get through my set, and when it's time to return to the dressing room, I bend to scoop my discarded clothes and bills off the stage. I scurry through the curtain and am immediately lifted off the floor and shoved against the wall. My eyes are squeezed shut, and when I open my mouth to scream, a large hand covers it.

"It's me darlin'."

My eyes fly open and Jackson stares back at me, a grin tugging at the corners of his mouth. My legs wrap around his waist, and his lips fuse to mine. I lose myself in the kiss, forgetting where we are.

He has me pinned so tightly that his hands are free, and he's got my wrists secured and raised above my head. I lock my ankles at the small of his back, and my hips buck, seeking contact with something, anything, that will bring me relief from the intense *need* burning between my legs.

When he pulls his mouth from mine, his eyes are dark, brooding, but his grin has widened. "Sorry 'bout that."

My breathing is labored, and I have no response.

"Watching you on stage, knowing what you taste like, what you feel like, is torture. And seeing other men stare at you, want you the way I do, is worse than death."

"I just have one question," I say.

"And hopefully I have an answer."

"Who was just kissing me? Jack or Jackson?" I raise my brow, curiosity getting the better of me.

"Both."

Jackson lowers me until my feet reach the floor. He takes his leather jacket off and covers my nude body. I inhale his scent as he wraps me up.

"I can live with that," I murmur.

"Go get dressed." He urges me away from him. "I've got a few things to take care of, and then we can get out of here."

He turns and walks away, leaving me standing there, staring, speechless. Butterflies dance in my stomach at what he's implying. I'm going home with him… again.

I strut into the dressing room, and Sapphire, along with four of the other girls, are standing there with expectant looks on their faces. Heat creeps up my neck and spreads over my face.

"What?" I ask as I pull my wig off and shake out my blonde locks.

"Girl, you've got some side hustle goin' on," Sapphire squeals, although her tone doesn't quite match the look on her face.

"Side hustle?"

"Yeah. You know, banging the help for extra dough. No wonder Mr. Vick likes you so much."

Is that what they think? That I'm some whore that'll spread her legs for a bit of cash? *Apparently.* With everything going on, I'm not sure I should set them straight. I don't know what they know about the escort side of things, and I'm not clear on how Jackson wants me to portray our *association* while at the club. Better to wait and talk to him about it.

I ignore their teasing and move to my locker. Jackson said he had a few things to take care of, so I take my time getting ready to go.

"Kitty Kat!"

I whirl around and come face to face with the man I fear the most. Mr. Vick never comes into the dressing room, unless it's before a performance to make sure we look 'fuckable'. My stomach drops to the floor. What could he possibly want? Certainly nothing good.

"That was quite the performance tonight," he snears with a cocked head and an arched brow. "Almost as if you were stripping for one man in particular."

I glance around the room, in hopes of finding an ally among vipers, but all of the other girls are gone. When had they left? Resigned to having to face Mr. Vick alone, I square my shoulders.

"And if I was?" I ask defiantly.

"If you were," he says, taking one step closer and threading his fingers through my hair until he's cupping the back of my head. "I'd have to remind you who you really belong to."

He wraps the blonde strands in his fist and yanks back. My scalp stings and tears gather in my eyes, but I refuse to let them fall.

"Have you forgotten about our deal?" he asks as he pulls

harder, my eyes almost unable to look at anything other than the ceiling.

I try to shake my head but am unable to move it. "No," I respond through clenched teeth.

"I own you, little gi—"

"What the fuck are you doing?"

Mr. Vick's grip is suddenly gone, and I reach up to rub the sore spot, staring at the man that has inflicted so much pain. Mr. Vick's eye twitches, and he slowly turns around to face off with Jackson.

"Excuse me?"

Jackson's eyes lock with mine as he speaks to Mr. Vick. "You said I could have her."

"I said you could *use* her while we sort other matters out. Are you telling me that Luciano accepted another arrangement?"

Jackson's eyes narrow as he shakes his head and turns his gaze on Mr. Vick. "No, not yet. But I've got a meeting set up with him."

I can't see Mr. Vick's face, but his body tenses at that bit of news. "Well… I guess we'll all just have to wait and see what happens then." He takes a step closer to Jackson. "In the meantime, I still own her. I agreed to her being your plaything, but under this roof, I'll do what I want to any of the girls, Kitty Kat included."

If murder had an expression, it would be the one Jackson's wearing as Mr. Vick walks away and out the door. When he's gone, air whooshes from my lungs and my body deflates. Jackson rushes to me and pulls me into his arms, his hands rubbing up and down my back.

"I'm sorry."

"What do you have to be sorry about?"

"I told you that you were safe, and he got to you." Jackson steps away from me and stares into my eyes.

"Jackson, I'm fine. I can handle a little hair pulling." My words betray the angst I'm feeling at my encounter with Mr. Vick.

"Oh yeah?" he asks as a sly smile appears. "Care to test that theory?"

I swat at his chest, chuckling. "You're impossible."

"Nah, not impossible." His expression sobers. "I'm done for the night. Let's get out of here."

He interlocks his fingers with mine and reaches behind me to snag my bag out of my locker, slamming it shut when it's slung over his shoulder. He tugs me toward the door, and I have no choice but to quickstep to keep up.

Jackson's phone rings just as he shuts the car door behind me. He stands near the hood while he takes the call. While he's handling his business, my own cell rings in my bag. I retrieve it, and a ball of dread forms in the pit of my stomach when I see the name on the screen.

"Mom, what's wrong?" I skip pleasantries because it's the middle of the night, and my mother wouldn't be calling me unless something was seriously wrong.

"Kyle's missing." Her voice has a nasal quality, like she's been crying.

"What?" I demand, throwing open the car door and putting the phone on speaker. I run to Jackson, not caring if I'm interrupting his call.

"Oh, sweetie," mom cries. "Your dad and I have been trying to get a hold of him since this morning, and he's not answering. Not calls or texts."

"Maybe he's at a party." I don't believe that. It isn't like Kyle not to respond to our mom. He's a mama's boy.

Jackson stares at me, but his expression isn't worried, and he puts his hand over the phone. "Katelyn, Kyle is fine. Hang up the phone." He returns to whoever he's talking to. "I gotta go."

"Kate, what do we do? Call the police?" my mom asks. That would have been my first phone call.

Jackson is shaking his head at the question my mom posed and mouths 'no cops'. I scramble to come up with a way to convince my mom that her precious son is alive and well and not to involve the police. Besides, Jackson is an FBI agent, which is better than a cop, right?

I come up empty and decide to take a new tactic. "Mom, is dad there? Can I talk to him."

Mom huffs but hands over the phone.

"Honey, it's dad." My father seems calmer than my mom, but that's no surprise. He's always had the cooler head. "You know how your mom is. She hasn't been able to reach him all day. I've reminded her that he's in college now and is probably busy."

Jackson's lips twitch, and I roll my eyes.

"Sir, you don't know me, but I'm a friend of your daughters." Jackson's voice is softer than usual, and it curls around me, taking away the chill of the night air. "My name is Jackson, and I'm an FBI agent." My eyes widen at his admission. "I assure you, Kyle is okay."

Jackson gives me an apologetic look, and my heart sinks. He knows more than he's willing to say to my father and apparently more than he's been willing to tell me.

"Kate, why are you with an FBI agent?" My father is concerned. I'm his little girl, and I have no doubt his mind immediately conjured up all of the worst case scenarios. "Are you in some kind of tr—"

"Jackson's my boyfriend," I blurt out and it's Jackson's turn to have wide eyes. His shocked expression quickly turns to one of approval.

"Oh." My dad takes a deep breath. "Well, then, you'll have to bring him to dinner sometime. I'd like to meet the fella that's spending time with my daughter."

"Sure, dad." I roll my eyes again and Jackson chuckles.

"Wait a sec." In my mind's eye, I can see my dad bristling, holding up his hand to stop whatever is going on around him. "How do you know that Kyle is okay? Why does the FBI know that Kyle is okay?"

"Mr. Dawson, Kyle is crashing at Katelyn's place." Jackson looks at me and shrugs. "He, uh, had a fight with his girlfriend and just wanted to get away for awhile."

"Girlfriend? We didn't even know he had a girlfriend." The gears are turning in my father's head. He's not quite convinced that Jackson's telling the truth.

"Neither did I," I rush to add. "Not until he showed up at my apartment."

"Something doesn't feel right."

"Dad, everything is fine. I promise." *Don't make a liar out of me, Jackson.*

"Well, if he's there, put him on the phone so he can talk to your mother. She's fit to be tied, and I'm afraid that's all that will help."

"We aren't at the apartment, sir. We're out grabbing some pizza. But when we get back, we'll have him call right away." Jackson's eyes bore into mine as he speaks.

He has so much explaining to do, and I'm beyond upset that, for some unknown reason, I'm lying through my teeth to my parents.

"Dad, we gotta go or we'll never get home."

"Right, okay." My father huffs out a breath. "Just have him call, Kate. So we can stop worrying."

"I will, dad." I hate lying to him, especially when he sounds so defeated. The entire situation sucks. "I love you. Tell mom I love her, too."

"We love you too, honey."

My father disconnects the call, and I lift the phone up to stare at the blank screen. My thoughts swirl at all of the possibilities. I want to demand that Jackson explain, but he's already on his phone again. I try to listen to what he's saying, but his voice sounds far away, muffled, which is weird because he's standing right next to me.

"We're on our way."

Those words somehow break through the fog, and suddenly, I'm floating outside my body, not at all in control of my actions. I'm pounding on Jackson's chest, my own heaving as I try to breathe through the anger, the confusion. Every emotion is flowing through my fists. Everything I've endured over the last few months, every fear, every catcall, every grimy hand that's touched my body, every article of clothing I've left on the stage, everything.

Jackson lets me hit him for a few minutes. He stands there, silently taking it, letting me get it all out. When my movements slow, he wraps his arms around me and holds me tight. I struggle against him, not wanting his comfort, not wanting his support, but he doesn't release me.

"Katelyn, I need you to calm down," he whispers against my hair. "I'm going to explain everything, and I'm going to take you to Kyle. But you need to calm down."

The mention of my brother's name is all it takes. I shove away from Jackson and storm to the car. I practically throw myself inside and slam the door behind me. Jackson doesn't make a move to join me. He tips his head to the sky and looks like he's carrying the weight of the world.

Good.

When he takes longer than I want, I lean across the seat and press the horn, which causes him to jump. He rounds the hood and gets in the car. He does something on his phone before cranking the engine and gunning it out of the parking lot.

After we're clear of the club, he tosses the phone in my lap. I ignore it.

"Dammit, pick up the phone and look at the picture." His hands are gripping the steering wheel so tightly that his knuckles are white. "You want answers, look at the fucking picture."

My hand shakes as I pick up the device. I don't want to see a picture. But I do want answers. When I see what he wants me to see, my lungs seize and my heart stops.

It's a picture of Kyle, tied to a chair, blood trickling down his face, with Stoner standing behind him with a gun pointed at the back of his head.

12

JACKSON

Katelyn's pale skin is visible beneath every streetlight we pass. That picture threw her for a loop, and she's been silent for most of the drive. I know I need to explain, but I'm kind of afraid to. Not because I'm afraid of her. No, I'm worried that the information I give her will ruin whatever is developing between us. Or was developing until about forty minutes ago.

I keep my focus on the road, only sneaking glances at her out of the corner of my eye. She already slapped my hand away when I tried to rest it on her thigh, so I won't be trying that again. For now.

"You said he was fine." Her voice is quiet in the dark car, barely audible with the sound of the road rushing beneath us.

I glance at her, and she still isn't looking at me. Her attention is on her lap, on her twisting hands.

"Darlin', Kyle *is* fine."

"Don't," she snaps and it's the first spark of, well, anything, I've seen since she looked at the photo. "You don't get to call me that. You don't get to be charming."

"And you don't get to be pissed because I did my job," I yell back.

Her head whips around, and she glares at me through narrowed eyes. Her body is wound tight, tension evident in her posture.

"And what exactly is your job, *Jack*?" She's baiting me, trying to piss me off with the use of my assumed identity. "Is your job to lie to me? To make me feel safe while you go behind my back and do God knows what? Is it your job to fuck your informants?" Her voice is getting louder, more desperate. "That's all I am, right? An informant? Some poor shmuck who was too stupid to see this," she waves her hand between us, "for what it is?"

Unable to stand her accusation slinging any longer, I jerk the wheel to the right and swerve to the side of the road, throwing the car in park as dust kicks up from the tires. For a split second it crosses my mind that this is a bad idea, that someone might see us, but a quick glance around reminds me of where we are. Some back road that no one travels unless they're going to Broken Rebel Brotherhood property. No one will see.

I throw my door open and rush around to her side of the vehicle. Fury is flowing through me, so I force myself to take a few deep breaths and calm the fuck down before I yank her out of her seat. She tries to lock the door, but I'm quicker.

She stumbles as I tug her toward me, and I grip her arms so she doesn't fall. She struggles for a minute or two but gives up when she realizes I'm not letting her go.

"You done?" I ask when it seems she's out of anger.

"Whatever," she mumbles and turns her head so she's not looking at me.

"That isn't an answer." I grip her chin and force her to face me. "Are you done slinging accusations? Yes or no?"

"Fine," she says, teeth clenched. "Yes, I'm done."

"Good. Now maybe you'll keep your mouth shut and let me speak." Her lips part, as if she wants to argue, but I stop her before she can even start. "Mouth. Shut."

She pulls away from me, and I let her. Her arms cross over her chest, and she starts tapping her foot. It takes every ounce of self control not to laugh at her little tantrum, but I manage.

"I'm going to talk. You're going to listen. That's how this is going to work."

I take a step back, putting some distance between us. Not because I want the distance but because I'm hoping she'll feel less threatened and remain a little calmer.

"I got that picture of your brother before we went into the club." Her mouth opens, and I hold up a hand. "No. Talking." Her mouth slams shut. "I handled it. He's safe. Shaken but safe."

Her bottom lip begins to tremble, betraying the calm indifference she's trying to project. No longer able to keep my distance, I step up to her and cup her face, rubbing my thumbs across her cheekbones.

"I kept it from you because I didn't want you to be scared. Yes, that was selfish. If you had known, you wouldn't have been able to get through your shift, and I needed you to be there, like nothing was out of the ordinary." Anger, false calm indifference, whatever you want to call it, morphs into sadness. "Katelyn, I can't screw this up. This case, it's important. Not just to the Bureau, but to me. But I also don't want to mess up whatever is happening here, with us."

"Nothing is happening," she says.

"You can deny it all you want." I let out a humorless chuckle. "Hell, you can pretend you hate me, but I know the truth." I take her hand and hold it to my chest, covering it with my much larger one. "Look, we've only been together, what, a day? But I've been watching you for months. I know you." She rolls her eyes. "I *know* you. And if you stop and think about it, you know me. At least the important stuff."

"Ha! I know your name and your profession. I don't know shit."

"You know I'm loyal. You know I'll protect you, no matter what. You know I'll do anything for you. You know the important things." When she just stares at me, I add, "You know we're phenomenal in bed together."

She snorts at that and quickly tries to hide it with a scowl.

"Sure, there are things we don't know, but there doesn't have to be. I want to know everything about you, and I want you to know everything about me. But I need you to trust me a little bit longer. Can you do that?"

Her arms drop to her sides as if they're lead weights she can no longer hold. She glances at the field next to the road and appears to be contemplating her answer. Suddenly, her gaze returns to me, and it's full of questions.

"You said that this case is important to you." She tilts her head. "Why?"

Of course she'd ask the one question I don't want to answer. Not because she doesn't deserve to know. She absolutely does. But it's an ugly answer, one that doesn't paint me in the best light.

"Revenge," I answer simply.

"Revenge? For what?"

I take a deep breath and brace myself for the look of pity my answer is sure to cause.

"Kevin Vick is responsible for the murder of my wife and son."

13

KATELYN

Murder? Wife, son?

Jackson made that statement, and then began to pace. I'm tracking his every movement, trying to wrap my mind around what he said. All of the anger, all of the hurt and feeling of betrayal fled the moment he uttered the words. Instead, all I feel is sadness. For him, for his family, and if I'm being honest, for me.

How could he ever have a relationship after something that horrific? How could I ever replace what he lost? Because that's what I am. A replacement. His second chance to get it right.

"Jackson," I call out to him, hoping he'll talk to me. Oh, how the tables have turned.

He stops pacing in front of me, his head hanging down. When he raises it, his eyes are glistening.

"Jackson, I'm so sorry for what happened to your family." I reach out and place my hand flat against his chest. "I can't even imagine what that was like. But I'm not them."

"Don't you think I know that?" he snaps.

"I don't know." I pull my hand away and shrug. "Do you?"

"Of course I do," he yells. "Don't mistake my actions, my feelings, for a desperate attempt at a do-over. That isn't what this is." His voice lowers and he's pleading. "You aren't their replacement. No one could ever be that. But Vick's already gotten away with this for too long and nothing will stop me from making sure he gets exactly what he deserves."

"Okay."

I turn toward the car to get back in, and he grips my forearm, spinning me around to face him.

"You can't stop this. Fuck, I can't stop this. I just want him to pay. I want to be happy again. I want—"

I touch my finger to his lips, shutting him up. "I said 'okay.'"

"What?" he demands. "What does that even mean?"

"I won't get in the way of whatever you need to do. I'll help you, just like I said I would. And when it's done, when this crusade for revenge is over, we can see what this is, where this goes." His eyes widen. "But not before. I can't be your ticket to solving the case and your girlfriend, or whatever. I can't be two different people. So," I take a deep breath, blow it out slowly. "I'll be whatever it is you need me to be, and we can sort out the rest later."

He doesn't look happy about what I'm saying, but he gives a tight nod. "Okay. Fair enough."

"Good. Now, take me to my brother."

~

"Kate?"

Kyle looks at me through swollen eyes. There's no trace of the blood I saw in the picture, but the evidence of what was done to him is there. In his broken stare, in his puffy eyes, in the red rings around his wrists from being tied up.

I rush to his side, gripping his hand in mine. I can't stop

the tears from falling down my cheeks, and I swipe at them. I'm the big sister. I'm supposed to be strong for him.

"Kate, I'm fine. Really."

"I'm so sorry, Ky," I mumble through my tears. "None of this would have happened if it weren't for me. I'm so sorry."

Kyle wraps his arms around my shoulders and holds me close. We've always been close, my brother and me. I protected him from monsters when he was little, and he protected me from assholes when he got older, despite being younger than me. We have a bond that most siblings covet, and the fact that he could have been ripped from existence physically hurts my heart.

"Ah, Kate, stop crying," he begs.

I can't staunch the flow of tears no matter how hard I squeeze my eyes shut. I'm aware of my brother, of Jackson standing on the other side of the room talking to two men he introduced as Griffin and Aiden. And even though I'm aware, it's like none of it exists. Everything happening around me is somehow separate from me.

"If you won't stop crying, can you at least wipe your nose? It's running and it's gross."

His teasing does the trick. I huff out a wet laugh and manage to stop crying. I grab his arm and wipe my nose on his sleeve, knowing it would gross him out even more. Like I said, great sibling bond.

"You're disgusting," he whines as he nudges me away from him.

"You still love me," I tease.

"Yeah, I do." He leans back against the couch. "So, care to enlighten me?" he asks and nods his head toward the other men in the room.

"Not really, but I will." I don't want to explain everything to him. I don't want to give him a reason to think less of me. "First, though, call mom and dad. They're freaking out."

Kyle rolls his eyes, but he takes my cell and calls our parents. I try to divide my attention between his conversation and Jackson's but I can't hear anything specific. When Kyle hands the phone back to me, he's got a smile tugging at his mouth.

"All good?" I ask.

"Yeah." He looks at me with suspicion in his eyes. "They told me how sorry they were that I had a fight with my girlfriend." I feel my cheeks heat up at his words. "I don't have a girlfriend."

"I had to tell them something!"

"At least tell me my girlfriend is pretty," he jokes.

"Well, duh. Nothing but the best for you, little brother."

"You're nuts, you know that?" He stands up and pulls me with him. "Now, big sister, tell me what the hell is going on here."

I stare at him, debating on how to tell him that his sister is a stripper, that she gets paid money to take her clothes off and let men ogle her through alcohol induced bloodshot eyes.

"She will." Jackson's hands settle on my shoulders, offering support. "But she's scared."

"Of what?" my brother asks incredulously and searches Jackson's face for answers. "Me?"

"No, not *of you*. She's afraid of what you'll think of her."

"Stop!" I shout, unable to listen to them have a conversation about me like I'm not even here. I whirl around on Jackson. "Thank you for trying to help, but I've got this." I turn back to Kyle. "Jackson's right, though. I've done things, seen things that I'm not proud of. I don't want you to hate me."

"Oh for god's sakes." Kyle throws his hands up. "You're my sister. I could never hate you. But I can be pissed, which is what I'm getting because you won't fucking talk."

"Watch your mouth."

"Fine."

Jackson and I speak at the same time. Kyle darts his eyes back and forth between the two of us, seeming unsure of how to proceed. The words I need to say are gathering in my mind, trying to organize themselves into something that will make sense.

"Kate, talk," Kyle urges.

"I'm a stripper." The words are out of my mouth so fast, and they seem to sucker punch Kyle in the stomach because he falls back against the couch, sagging down into the cushion, his breath whooshing out of him.

He looks up at me, and all I see is the little boy who needed me to 'kill' the monsters under his bed before he could fall asleep. I force myself to continue.

"College is expensive, student loans need paid back, and jobs are hard to come by." I shrug, as if that makes all the sense in the world. At one time, it had. Now, not so much. "Brandie got me the job and… *things* happened."

"What things?"

I proceed to tell him the same story I told Jackson about how I got stuck working at The White Lily, how Brandie was sold. I tell him everything. Jackson fills in some holes for me but otherwise stays silent, letting me tell my story.

"Jesus," Kyle mutters when I'm done.

"The men that got to you are Vick's men," Jackson tells him. "I'm not sure why he sent them after you, but I'm guessing it was a way to keep Katelyn in line."

"I was already 'in line'!" I shout. "I've done everything he's ever asked of me."

Up until this point, Jackson has stood behind me, but at my outburst, he steps around me, standing between me and Kyle, and grabs my hands, squeezing them tight. His gaze doesn't waver from mine.

"Darlin', Vick has plans for you."

I rear back, try to break free of his hold. Kyle lunges up from his spot on the sofa.

"What the fuck kind of plans?" Kyle demands.

That's when it hits me. Brandie was sold to pay off a debt. Mr. Vick forced me to stick around to pay off mine.

"He has more debt, doesn't he? I'm going to be his payment."

I search Jackson's eyes for something, anything that will prove me wrong. There's nothing there.

"He's going to sell me."

14

MR. VICK

"What the hell happened?"

Jett and Stoner are quickly becoming my least favorite people. I gave them one job. One fucking job, and they couldn't do it. Again. Not only that, but they both look like boys who got the shit beat out of them in the schoolyard.

"Sir, we were ambushed. We had the kid, but—"

"I don't want your fucking excuses!" My fist connects with my desk making pens bounce, and spit flies from my mouth.

I stand to my full height and, not for the first time, wish I had another seven or eight inches to intimidate with. Sweat is pouring down my spine as I smooth my hands down the sides of my jacket and try to project more calm than I feel. I don't have time for this curveball if I want to get Luciano off my ass.

"Can you get him back?" I ask, already knowing the answer by the look in their eyes.

"Sir, we can try." Stoner glances at Jett before continuing.

"The thing is, these were no ordinary men. The entire thing felt off."

"How so?" I ask, intrigued and maybe a little concerned.

"It was clear they had a mission: rescue Kyle." Stoner's face is a ruddy red, betraying his calm tone. He's as pissed as I am, although for entirely different reasons, I'm sure. "Why didn't Kyle recognize them if that's the case? And more importantly, why did they let us go?"

"That does seem odd," I concede, although I'm too furious at this turn of events to really consider the answers to those questions. "I'm sure it's nothing. I have a lot of enemies."

"Or," Stoner takes a deep breath. "It means we have a leak."

I bristle at the suggestion because not only is it intolerable, it also means I didn't do as good a job vetting my employees as I thought.

"Jett, what do you think?" He's been noticeably silent since walking into my office.

"I think you have a lot of enemies, sir."

"Are we just going to ignore the fact that your head of security isn't here and hasn't been here as much as he should be since he fucked Kitty Kat?" Stoner leans on my desk, hands flat and arms flexed.

"It's been a day," Jett scoffs. "It's not like he's been cock deep in pussy for weeks."

Stoner whirls on Jett. "So what? He's never given a shit about the girls, not really. At least not enough to take 'em home more then once. Why now? Why her?" Stoner pivots back to me. "I'm tellin' ya boss, there's something there."

"You just don't like the guy because he held a gun to your head," Jett says to Stoner's back.

I listen to their exchange in silence. I hear what Stoner is saying, but I just don't see it. Jack has been loyal to me for a year, and he was thoroughly checked out before I gave him the opportunity to become my head of security. An opportunity too good to pass up. Besides, Jett makes a valid point. Stoner doesn't like it when someone gets the drop on him. His ego is bruised. That's all.

Still, I'm not stupid and I can't completely ignore his concerns. I make a mental note to keep an eye on Jack for a while. Just until I know for sure if he is friend or foe. Jett and Stoner are still bickering about Jack when I walk to my office door and throw it open.

"That'll be all," I shout over their raised voices.

Both stare at me in shock at being dismissed in the middle of what they seem to consider a great debate.

"Sir, what is our next move?" Stoner asks.

"Nothing."

"Nothing, sir?"

"Do you have a hearing problem on top of your utter incompetence?" I don't give either of them a chance to say anything. "You'll know what the next move is when I want you to know. Now, get out!"

They both exit my office with scowls on their faces. I didn't lie to them. I will tell them what their next move is when I want to.

I just have to figure out what that is first.

15

JACKSON

"I'm going with you."

My meeting with Luciano is less than twenty four hours away, and the last thing I need to deal with right now is Katelyn's stubbornness. She can't be there. Not if I want to be able to focus on my job.

"No, you're not." I smile at her to soften my words. "Katelyn, this isn't up for debate."

"You're right, it's not up for debate," she fires back. "I'm going. It's up to you whether we arrive at the same time or if I'm a minute or two later."

I shove my hands in my pockets and rock back on my heels. Katelyn is infuriating, but she's also determined, confident, and I can't fault her for that.

"Look, when Slade gets here, we'll discuss it further." I glance at my watch. "He should be here any minute."

We're in a little dive bar on the opposite side of the city from the club. It's the middle of the afternoon so there are very few patrons and absolutely zero chance of anyone connected to Vick strolling through the door. Kevin Vick has a routine, and he likes to stick to it. He's predictable, or so I thought up until the last few days.

Slade and I have been meeting here once a week since the operation started, always sitting at the same dark corner booth. We'd chosen this particular booth the first time because the light hanging from the ceiling above the table hadn't been working, and apparently the owner didn't give a shit because it still doesn't. Hell, for all I know, everyone thinks that Slade and I are meeting up as secret lovers, always the same day of the week and the same time. As far as I'm concerned, better they think that than know the truth.

The door opens, casting a beam of sunlight to shine through the hazy space. The two drunks sitting at the bar glance over their shoulders at the newcomer, and when they spot Slade, they return to nursing their beers. Slade strolls over to the booth and comes to a halt next to the worn table, shifting his eyes between Katelyn and me. He shakes his head and turns to grab a chair from the table behind him, flipping it around and straddling it.

"You must be Katelyn Dawson." He greets her without acknowledging me and sticks his hand out to shake hers. "I'm Slade."

Katelyn shakes his hand, and I can't help but notice the way her eyes widen as she takes him in. Jealousy snakes through me, and I have to resist the urge to shove a fist down his throat. It's not his fault women love him and are attracted to him. But it is fucking annoying.

"So," Slade breaks contact with Katelyn and shifts to face me. "Catch me up."

I launch into everything that's happened over the last few days, aware that I should have kept him in the loop from the get-go. Katelyn narrows her eyes at me when I leave out the mention of Micah, Griffin and Aiden, but for some reason, she says nothing, and I'm grateful. The Broken Rebel Brotherhood doesn't need the FBI sniffing around.

"That's about it," I say when I finish filling him in. "I have this meeting with Luciano and I'm hoping we can wrap this shit up within a few more days."

"I think you're leaving out some pretty huge details." Slade glances at Katelyn.

"No, he told you everything." Katelyn shakes her head.

Slade's face gives nothing away, unless you know him, which I do. His jaw is hard, the vein in his neck is pronounced, there's a tick at the corner of his eye. He's fucking pissed, and he's trying to reign it in.

"Everything except the fact that he's sleeping with the job."

At the same time Katelyn rears back, as if physically slapped, I lean forward and grab Slade by the lapels of his jacket.

"It's none of your fucking business who I sleep with," I snarl.

"That's where you're wrong." He reaches up and tears my hands from him before shoving them away from his body. "You made it my business when you decided that your one-night-stand was important enough to lie to me for."

Katelyn scoots across the seat and stands, her face pale and her eyes wide. "I'm just gonna go to the restroom." With that, she practically runs from the table and disappears behind the ancient swinging saloon doors that separates the main area from the dim hallway where the bathrooms are.

"What the fuck is wrong with you?"

"What's wrong with me?" Slade counters. "You're the one banging the stripper and screwing the case."

"You don't know what you're talking about."

"No? So you haven't slept with her?" He quirks a brow at me.

I have no answer to that. At least not one he's going to like.

"Jackson, we've worked together for a little over a year now. We're partners. Don't you think I deserve the truth?"

"You want the truth? Fine, here it is." I point toward the doors that Katelyn walked through. "That girl is incredible. Sure, she's made some bad life choices, but she's paying for them. She's helping me bring Vick down even though she knows it may end badly. She does what needs to be done. And yes, I've slept with her, but she put a stop to it until the case is over, so you don't have to worry that my dick will fuck this up. She won't let it."

"Well, shit." Slade straightens and thrusts his fingers through his hair. "You're serious about her, aren't you?"

"Look, Slade, I don't expect you to understand but when you get to be my age—"

"You're thirty! Not exactly a wise old man."

"When you've been dealt the hand I have," I continue as if he hadn't spoken. "You learn to never take a single second for granted."

Slade stares at me with questions in his eyes. I've never talked to him about my wife and son, but I know he knows. I do have a personnel file and no doubt he was given the opportunity to read it, just like I read his, when we were first partnered together. He's never brought up Melinda and Ben, and I've never brought up his penchant for short love-em-and-leave-em marriages. Guys just don't talk about that shit.

Slade gives a curt nod. "Just quit keeping shit from me, man."

"Fair enough."

Katelyn returns and slides into the booth, eyeing us both warily before settling her gaze on Slade. "We good?"

"Yeah. We're good." Slade chuckles and the tension in the air dissipates.

"Great." Katelyn's lips tug up at the corners. "Now can you tell this dumb-ass," she nods her head toward me, "that I'm going with him to his meeting with Luciano?"

"I already told you that's not going to happen," I snap. "Tell her, Slade. It's not safe."

"You said we'd talk about it when Slade got here. He's here. Let's talk."

"I told you that to shut you up." As soon as the words leave my mouth, I regret them.

Katelyn's out of the booth so fast, but Slade grabs her wrist to stop her from storming away. She glares at his hand, and daggers shoot from her eyes. Her chest is heaving, and her face is red. Slade drops her arm and puts his hands up in a gesture of surrender.

"Katelyn, sit down." When she doesn't move, he adds, "Please."

Katelyn returns to her seat, but she's pissed and refuses to look at me. Slade gives her a minute to calm down and directs his attention to me.

"What exactly is this meeting about?"

"It's about me!" Katelyn snaps.

I roll my eyes at her outburst. "Vick has been using women as payment for his debts." I ignore the angry pout on Katelyn's face and focus on Slade. "He's already used Katelyn's best friend, Brandie, and now he wants to use Katelyn as his next payment."

"Like I said, it's about me." When I glare at Katelyn, she snaps her mouth shut.

"And you're meeting with him, why? I mean, Vick's obviously kept this part of his enterprise a secret from you. Why bring you in now?"

I take a deep breath, knowing Slade isn't going to like the answer. Neither is Katelyn, for that matter. "I staked my claim." I shrug. "I knew I needed to stay with Katelyn as much as possible, so I told him I wanted her to myself, to play with." I wince at my callous words. "He agreed that I could have her *if* I worked something out with Luciano. I agreed."

"Of course you did." Slade sighs and glances at Katelyn. "Why do you want to go? Sounds like it'd be smarter if you didn't. Certainly less dangerous."

"I promised Jackson I'd help him." Katelyn's temper has cooled, and in its place is determination. "And this is about me, so…"

"It's not about you, darlin'," I say when she doesn't continue. "This has nothing to do with you and everything to do with power, control. You're a product, nothing more. At least to them."

"But I can help. I know I can. You've gotta let me help."

"Maybe she should go." Both Katelyn and I whip our heads to look at Slade. He shrugs. "Think about it, Jackson. Luciano wants Katelyn and—"

"Which is stupid because he's never even met me," Katelyn interrupts.

"Even better." A grin tugs at Slade's mouth. I know that grin. It's the one he gets when he's got an idea, and I'm fairly certain it's going to be one I don't like. "At the end of the day, all Luciano wants is payment. He thinks he wants Katelyn, but what if you convince him he doesn't?"

"What do you mean?"

"Men like Luciano, they want power over people, they want to be able to control the situation. He wants a woman he can bend to his will. Show him that Katelyn isn't that woman."

"It's perfect." Katelyn smiles for the first time since returning from the bathroom.

"It's dangerous," I counter. I see what Slade is saying, and it makes sense, but I don't want Katelyn anywhere near this monster.

She strips for a monster almost every night and she's managed just fine. She'll have you this time.

"Jackson, I get that you don't like this, but the investigation has to take priority." Slade's calm only amps up my rage at this entire line of conversation. "You'll be there to protect her. I'll be close enough, listening in. What could go wrong?"

"Everything," I push out through clenched teeth.

Katelyn reaches across the table and lays her hands on mine. "You wanted my help. You *needed* my help. So let me help."

I flip my hands over, palms up, and rub my thumbs over her knuckles. How is it that a man can have the world by the balls one minute and the next, the world's balls are suffocating him?

"You do everything exactly how I tell you. You follow my lead and you never leave my side." I look her in the eyes, never letting mine waver. "You agree to my terms and you can go."

"I'll do everything exactly as you say."

"Fine." I can't deny that the light that enters her eyes almost makes the concession worth it.

I force myself to shift from concerned one-time lover to all-business FBI agent. I drop Katelyn's hands and sit back, although I don't let the tension ease from my body. I look at Slade out of the corner of my eye and he looks smug, but I ignore it, instead choosing to focus on a course of action.

"Let's plan."

16

KATELYN

You can do this. You can do this. You can do this.

I repeat the mantra on a loop as Jackson leads me toward the warehouse door that Luciano is behind. My hands are bound together by a zip tie, although it's fairly loose so I can get out of it if I need to. When Jackson opens the steel door, my brain goes silent. The mantra stops and so do I, digging in my feet and refusing to walk.

"I can't do this." I shake my head back and forth and try to pull away from Jackson. "I'm s-sorry. I thought I could, but I can't."

Jackson urges me back through the door and lets it close behind him, providing me with a barrier again. He cups my cheeks and bends so he's at eye level with me.

"Katelyn, you've got this." He kisses my forehead. "I'm going to be with you the whole time."

"You were right. This is dangerous. I shouldn't be here." Why didn't I listen to him? Why did I have to push to be included. *Stupid, stupid, stupid.*

"It *is* dangerous. I'm not going to deny that. Darlin', you're stronger than you think."

I let his voice wash over me, let his words sink in. If Jackson believes in me, then I can too. I can't quite force words out of my mouth, so I nod, letting him know I'm good. We can continue now.

"That's my girl."

He drops his hands and turns back to the door. I can see his muscles ripple beneath his shirt as he opens it and pulls me along with him. I can't help but look around the large space, taking in the shipping containers, the wooden palettes piled high, and rows upon rows of shelving.

At first glance, it reminds me of what I would expect an Amazon warehouse to look like. But this isn't Amazon. No Prime deals, no two-day shipping, no one-stop online shopping. Nope. This is a place where the bad guys get the products they sell on the streets. Credit card not required.

"That's far enough."

The voice startles me, and I almost run into Jackson's back. I take a deep breath and step to his side, forcing myself to face the source of the command. When I catch sight of who I can only assume is Luciano, I have to stifle a snort.

He's just as bad as Vick. Tiny little man with a big man ego. His hair is thinning, and the dye job is so bad it almost looks like someone took a can of black spray paint and pointed it at his nearly bald head and closed their eyes, hoping to get it right.

"Mr. Vick sends his regards." Jackson's tone is all business.

"I'm sure he does." The man walks toward us, and it takes everything in me not to slink back. He sticks out his hand to shake Jackson's. "I'm Saul. You must be Jack."

"That's right." Jackson pumps his hand a few times and then pulls away. "As I said when I called, I want…"

The rest of Jackson's words fade away. His lips are still moving, he's still talking, but I don't hear a damn thing. All I can focus on is the way Luciano is leering at me, a disgusting grin on his face and evil in his eyes. Jackson finally seems to notice that no one is listening to him, and he closes his mouth.

"Vick has good taste," Luciano sneers, licking his lips.

"You'd think," Jackson barks out a laugh.

I glance between Luciano and Jackson, reading the expression on Jackson's face, silently reminding me of the plan. Something in me shifts, and I let all of my disgust, all of my fear, all of my anger rush to the surface. Before I can think twice, I swirl the saliva around in my mouth, making sure there's plenty, and spit in Luciano's face.

Luciano stares at me with a shocked expression, my spit clinging to his cheek. He slowly reaches into his pocket and pulls out a handkerchief. *People still use those?* When he's cleaned his face, he glares at me before looking at Jackson.

"Is this a joke?"

"No joke," Jackson assures him. "Mr. Vick says you want Kitty Kat, and he thinks she'd be a good fit. Problem is, he doesn't know her that well. I do. That's why I asked for this meeting."

"And?"

"With all due respect, sir, I'm Mr. Vick's head of security. It's my job to keep him safe, as well as to protect his business interests." Jackson glances at me, and even though I know it's an act, I can't help the fear that skates up my spine at his expression. "Handing over Kitty Kat to you is not going to keep him safe. It's going to make him a target." Luciano tilts his head in question. "Kitty Kat's a stupid bitch. I've tried to, shall we say, *coax* the attitude out of her. So far, that's proved difficult, but—"

"Fuck you both!" I shout and struggle against the binding

at my wrists, ignoring the pain. I have to nail this if Luciano is going to believe a word Jackson says.

"Ah, yes. She's got some fight in her." Luciano traces a fingertip down my cheek, and when he reaches my chin, he drops his arm and turns to walk away. After he takes a few steps, he peers over his shoulder. "Follow me."

Jackson chances a quick glance at me before dragging me behind him to follow. We walk though the warehouse and go through another steel door, down a long hallway, coming to a stop at a flight of stairs. In order to descend the steps, one must first pass through the big metal detector that makes up the doorframe. Next to that, along the wall, is a locker, like the ones you see lining the halls of a high school.

"I'm gonna have to ask you to leave your phone and your weapons." Luciano tilts his head to indicate the locker. "Neither are permitted past this point."

"I don't think so," Jackson says, steel lacing his tone.

"Your choice, Mr. Duffy." Luciano shrugs and shifts his black eyes to me. "I'm sure I can beat her into submission and then take my troubles out of Mr. Vick later."

Jackson bristles and I fear he's going to snap, forget the objective. He manages to gain control and slips his gun out of its holster and his cell out of his pocket. He tosses both into the locker. Luciano does the same and then leads us down the stairs. The lower we go, the colder the air gets. Goosebumps break out over my skin, and I can't stop the shiver that races through me.

When we reach the bottom, there's yet another steel door, this one with a keypad to the right. Luciano enters a code, and the door swings open. Shock settles over me at the sight before us.

This is not some kingpin's dungeon. This isn't the lair of a killer. This isn't a human trafficker's home base. It doesn't even come close to the hell I was expecting.

What lies before me is an underground palace, complete with bright colors, crystal chandeliers, and marble tiled floors.

What the hell?

17

JACKSON

"Not what you were expecting?"

I resist the urge to respond with 'not even a little bit' and instead shrug my shoulders.

"I had no idea what to expect." But no, a *home* wasn't even on the list of possibilities.

Luciano walks to the center of the space—I refuse to call it a foyer—and taps his foot on a gold button that protrudes from the floor. He takes a step back as the marble tiles separate and a small table rises, with an old-school rotary phone atop it.

Luciano dials one number, holds the receiver up to his ear, and then politely asks whoever is on the other end to bring drinks to the library. When he replaces the receiver, the table disappears back into the floor.

What the actual fuck?

I wish Slade were here. He's not going to fucking believe me when I tell him about it.

"Mr. Luciano," I begin.

"Saul, please."

"Okay... Saul." *I'm in the fucking twilight zone.* "If you don't mind, I'd like to get down to business."

"Don't kid yourself. This is business."

Luciano walks away, leaving us to do nothing but follow, again. We enter what I assume is the library, and standing in the middle of the room, next to an ornate looking desk, is a woman. A gorgeous woman with long red hair, wide eyes and a heart shaped mouth. I try to end my inspection at her face, but it's damn near impossible because she's standing there, a shocked expression playing across her features, naked.

I hear Katelyn's sharp intake of breath, and before I know what's happening, she's running to the woman and throwing her arms around her neck. I instantly regret not securing the zip ties tighter. So much for doing what I say and not leaving my side.

"What's the meaning of this?" Luciano barks.

Katelyn's ugly crying, or I imagine she is. I can't see her face while it's buried in the woman's neck. The woman doesn't move an inch, doesn't hug her back, but I can't miss the single tear that rolls down her cheek.

Ah, this must be Brandie.

I'm stunned. Speechless. I know I should stop Katelyn, order her to step away, but I can't. What happens next jars me out of my stupor, but not before it seems to start in agonizingly slow motion.

"You monster!" Katelyn screams as she launches herself at Luciano.

She claws at his face, kicks, punches, all the while wailing that she's going to kill him. I race forward to pull her off of him and am surprised at her strength. She struggles against me until she hears the click.

At the sound of a gun being cocked, she freezes. I look to

my left and see a man in a black suit pointing his weapon at her head. Rage sears my veins.

"No weapons. That's what you fucking said." My fury is directed at Luciano who is now sporting a sinister grin, made even worse by the bleeding scratches Katelyn inflicted.

"I did." He uses the same handkerchief from earlier and wipes at the blood. "But all bets were off when this *thing* started attacking me." He tilts his head to indicate Katelyn before turning to the suit with the gun. "Thank you, Jimmy. You can leave us."

Jimmy maintains his stance for a moment before lowering his weapon and leaving the room. Brandie still hasn't moved, despite the chaos around her.

"Why did you bring us down here?"

"I can see why you thought I'd be disappointed in Kitty Kat," he says, ignoring my question. "Don't get me wrong, I like a little fight in them, but not so much that they can't be broken."

He moves to sit behind his desk, linking his hands behind his head.

"This one here," he tilts his head to indicate Brandie. "She was weak. Fought for all of two minutes before she was cowering at my feet."

Katelyn stiffens at his words but doesn't speak. Her head shifts to Brandie, who lowers her eyes to the floor.

"I have a proposition for you, Mr. Duffy."

"And what would that be?" Something about the tone of his voice has tension coiling my muscles.

"I'll forfeit Kitty Kat as payment *if* Mr. Vick agrees to give me forty percent of any and all future profits from The White Lily."

"He'll never go—"

"I'm not done." Luciano leans forward, bracing his elbows

on the polished cherry wood desk. "I want forty percent plus access to all of the girls."

I whistle at his audacity, although he probably has a right to be cocky. He's clearly got more money than Vick, and despite the image he's portraying right now, he's a major player in the crime world. There is no way in hell that Vick will go for this, but Luciano doesn't need to know that yet.

"If he doesn't agree?"

"He will." Luciano smiles. "Because if he doesn't, I'll kill him and take what I want. Kitty Kat included. I can always have Jimmy break her, although it isn't quite as fun for me that way."

The thought of anyone 'breaking' Katelyn turns my stomach. I fight the urge to laugh in his face because I'll die before I let anything happen to her. Instead, I give him what he wants to hear, the words burning like acid on my tongue.

"I'll see what I can do."

"I'll give you one week. If I don't hear from you at the end of that time, I'll assume Vick said no and take it from there."

I nod, my mind racing a million miles a second, trying to come up with how I'm going to present this to my boss, convince him this is a smart move. Vick thinks he's at the top of the criminal food chain, but he doesn't even come close to Luciano.

"I'll be in touch."

I grip Katelyn's arm, rougher than I intended to, and try to turn her around so we can get out of this place. She digs in her feet and stares at Brandie. It's all I can do not to pull her close, assure her that we'll get Brandie, save her from this chameleon. Just as I'm about to force her to leave, she turns her attention to Luciano.

"You're a sick bastard, and I will make sure you rot in hell."

She tries to pull away from me, tries to lunge at him, but I manage to stop her and get her to turn toward the door. As we make our way out of the office, I hear Luciano's laugh echo behind us. As we reach the door that will lead us back to the warehouse, the unmistakable sound of a whip against flesh, followed by a piercing scream, bounces off the walls.

Motherfucker.

~

"We can't just leave her!"

With every step we take to safety, Katelyn's temper builds. Her body becomes rigid, and she tries to dig in her heels. I ignore her statement and continue to propel her forward, toward the warehouse exit.

I'd collected my gun and phone from the locker. The former is cocked and ready, while the latter is tucked into my pocket. Afraid we won't make it out of here if Katelyn keeps putting up a fight, I lift her up and toss her over my shoulder like a flour sack. She pounds on my back and yells at me to put her down, but I don't, not until we get outside and are standing next to the car we came in.

I lower her until her feet hit the ground, and she immediately whirls around and hurls the contents of her stomach onto the gravel lot. I pull her hair out of her face and rub her back, hating the toll this entire day has taken on her. When her puking ceases, she straightens and drags the back of her hand across her mouth to wipe it clean.

"Feel better?" I ask, knowing that no amount of vomiting is going to expel the last hour from her.

Rather than answer, she looks at me with so much hatred that I'm tempted to go back inside and do whatever it takes to get Brandie. Unfortunately, that's not an option right now. What Katelyn needs to realize is that I don't like it any more than she does.

STARK REVENGE

She gets in the car and slams the door. I take a few deep breaths before joining her. As we pull out of the parking lot, I reach over to grab her hand, and she pulls away, scooting as close to the door as she can without throwing it open and jumping out of the car.

"You can't ignore me forever." I sigh when she doesn't look my way.

The drive to The White Lily is tense and silent. The last thing I want to do is take her there, but we both have jobs to do. When we reach our destination, I cut the engine and turn in my seat to face Katelyn. Her posture is rigid, and she's staring out her window, looking at anything but me.

"Katelyn, please don't do this," I beg.

Her head whips around, and she narrows her eyes at me. "How many times do you think Brandie has said those words to him? One time, ten times? Or did he *break* her so quickly that those words aren't even in her vocabulary anymore?"

"I don't know," I answer her the only way I know how. "I don't know a lot of things, but the one thing I do know is I won't let anyone hurt you."

"I'm already hurt, Jackson." Her body seems to deflate, leaving her sad, which is worse in my opinion. "Brandie is my best friend and she's gone." When I open my mouth to contradict her, she holds up a hand. "No, she's gone. She might physically be alive, but what makes her *her* doesn't exist anymore."

I have no response to that. There is nothing I can say that will make this okay. There is nothing I can do to turn back time and make it so she never experiences any of this.

Would you want to? If you were able to, would you turn back the clock and possibly never have her in your life?

Yes. I would. Because that's what you do when you love someone. You make their life better even if it means yours is worse.

And you think you love her?

I do love her. When you've suffered as much as I have, when tragedy has taken everything important to you and turned it to ash, you tend to take life by the balls and live it, savoring every minute as if it could be your last.

"Jackson, promise me something." Katelyn's quiet voice pulls me from my thoughts.

"Darlin', I'd promise you the moon if I could."

"I don't want the moon. I want this to be over. I want my best friend back. I want my life back. Just… promise me you'll do everything you can to make that happen."

Every part of me screams to not make a promise I'm not certain I can keep, but as I told her, I'd promise her the moon if I could.

"I promise."

She nods once and then exits the vehicle, closing the door behind her. Without looking back, she walks into work, set on doing what needs to be done. I should be concerned that she'll have a hard time keeping up appearances, but for some odd reason, I'm not even a little worried.

Katelyn's strong, stronger than she thinks. She's a fighter. She's going to get what she wants and help me get what I need.

An arrest.

Revenge.

Her.

18

KATELYN

My hips undulate to the music, moving to a beat I don't even hear. Jackson has yet to make an appearance at his usual table. In fact, his table is taken. Jett and Stoner are there, leaning back in their chairs, seemingly without a care in the world.

Stoner has a slimy grin on his face as he watches me dance and every once in a while his hand goes to his junk. Thankfully, I already threw up the contents of my stomach, and I haven't been able to eat anything else since. Otherwise, I'd be giving a very different show tonight.

Jett doesn't look as vile. He's watching, staring, but there's no smile, no hint of anything to indicate he's enjoying what he sees. That almost makes him scarier than Stoner. At least with Stoner, I know what seems to make him tick. With Jett, I've got nothing.

When the song ends, I collect my clothes and the money thrown at me, and head back to the dressing room. The other girls are there, but I don't talk to them. I want to. I want to tell them to run for their lives, get out of this place while they still can, but I don't. Instead, I let them go about their night like everything is the same, like there isn't a greater than average chance they're going to be sold to a rich slimeball, used as a bargaining chip in a dangerous game.

"Bitch, you better snap out of it," Sapphire steps up beside me, staring back at me from our reflections in my mirror. "This doom and gloom attitude is messin' with my mojo."

"Sorry," I mumble and force a smile.

"What's wrong?" She tilts her head and rests her hands on her hips.

"Nothing. Just tired I guess."

"Well, snap out of it," she demands before walking away.

I pull off my wig and toss it on the counter, finger combing my hair with my free hand. I grab the make-up remover and scrub at my face, erasing any trace of Kitty Kat. Katelyn finally emerges, but she's not the same. She's forever changed by what she saw today.

"Kitty Kat, let's go."

Jackson's voice booms across the dressing room, and I whirl around to face him. He's standing in the doorway, jeans and worn leather jacket hugging his body. His arms are crossed over his chest, his feet braced apart. I know I told him that nothing could happen between us until the case was over, but seeing him now, all alpha, makes me want to forget the rule I imposed.

I grab my bag from my locker and follow him out of the building. He doesn't say another word until we're halfway to the car, at which time he turns around and frames my face in his hands, fusing his lips to mine.

The shock only lasts a second before I give in and kiss him back. I wrap my fingers around his wrists, hanging on for dear life. He finally pulls back and stares into my eyes.

"I needed that," he says as he rests his forehead on mine.

"Me too."

Just then Jackson's phone rings and he steps back to

answer it. He nods his head as he listens to whoever is on the other end. After telling them that we're on our way, he shoves his phone in his pocket and drags me the rest of the way to the car.

"Who was that?" I ask when he starts the engine.

"Slade." He maneuvers out of the lot and heads toward the interstate, the opposite direction from his place. "Higher ups are getting antsy. We've gotta figure something out to bring this to an end. Quick."

"I don't understand." I shake my head at him. "I mean, how can you end the investigation if you don't have what you need? Don't you need more to put Vick behind bars for longer than a few hours?"

"Of course we do," he snaps. He glances at me and smiles to soften his irritation. "It's not up to me though."

"What about Luciano? What about Brandie?"

When he doesn't answer, I know that he may not be able to keep his promise. I also know he'll do everything he can to try.

He keeps his attention on the road, hyperfocused on the task of driving. There's little traffic, but you'd think we were traveling at rush hour the way he's concentrating. We arrive at our destination, a twenty-four hour truck stop about forty-five miles from the club.

"Why are we here?"

Jackson shrugs. "This is where I was told to go. Food's good, too."

I follow him inside and he navigates around the tables to a booth in the back. Slade is sitting there, a chocolate shake and a plate of fries in front of him. There are already two glasses of water at the place settings across from him. Jackson and I slide in, and Slade wastes no time getting to the point.

"We need to make an arrest. We've got forty-eight hours to make it happen."

"It's not enough time." Jackson slams his fist on the table, rattling the silverware. Fortunately, the place isn't busy.

"No kidding." Slade shoves a few fries in his mouth and then speaks around them. "But you've had a year, and they either want results or they want to pull the plug on the whole thing."

"Slade, we're so close to not only nailing Vick, but Luciano, too. Fucker's smart but I know I can get him."

"I have no doubt but, Jackson, Vick's the target. Only Vick and his operation."

"Yeah, well, after tonight, the two operations aren't mutually exclusive." Jackson heaves a sigh and leans back against the cracked red leather.

"He went for it?" I ask excitedly. "Vick really agreed to the terms?"

"He did."

"You don't seem happy about that." In fact, he looks like this is the worst possible outcome.

"I'm not." He thrusts his fingers through his hair. "Why is he willing to do this? What does he get from it, other than to keep breathing. It just doesn't feel right."

"Maybe not, but it won't matter in a few days. We'll take down Vick and then we can go after Luciano." Slade looks excited, and I wish I could feel that way. I wish that Jackson shared his enthusiasm.

"The good news is Vick wants a meeting with Luciano tomorrow night." Jackson takes a deep breath before continuing. "He invited Luciano to the club. He's got something up his sleeve, but I can't figure out what."

"This is perfect," Slade exclaims. "They'll be in the same place, talking business. And when one of them slips up and says something stupid, we'll move in and get them both."

"You think it's going to be that easy?" Jackson leans across the table, his jaw granite-hard. "They haven't gotten to where they are by being stupid. Vick is very careful when he discusses business. Why do you think this has been so hard?"

"That's what we have you for." Slade glances at me. "And her."

"No!" Jackson's fists slam against the formica table. "Absolutely not. We've already involved her in too much."

I place my hand on Jackson's arm and squeeze. "Jackson, let me do this."

"Fuck no."

"Man, she's already going to be there. It's where she works."

"I don't care," Jackson snaps. "She can call off. Say she's sick or something. I'm not doing a fucking thing with her in that building."

"It's not up to you," I whisper. His head whips around, and he pins me with his stare. "I have to be there and you know that. I've never once called off and doing so now would only cause Vick to be suspicious."

Anguish settles over his features. He knows I'm right and he hates everything about that.

"I'm not going to be able to worry about you when this goes down. I'll be arrested just like everyone else. You'll be arrested. That's how this will work because it has to look real. I won't be one of the good guys during this, not as far as anyone at the club is concerned."

"I can make sure Katelyn's protected," Slade says. "I'll make sure that everyone on our side knows what she looks like, knows to be gentle with her." He glances at me. "But you will have to be arrested, and I can't promise what anyone not on our side will do."

"Will I have to stay in jail?" I ask, my stomach turning at the thought of having to be stuck in a cell with anyone.

"Not for long. You'll be booked, put in a cell for a while. As soon as Jackson or I can, we'll get you out. Make it look like you made bail or something. Few hours, tops."

I look at Jackson, gauging his reaction to this. It's exactly what I expect. Quiet, resigned, furious.

"If we're going to do this, if we're going to make this work, we need a rock solid fucking plan," Jackson growls. "We prepare for every eventuality. I don't just want Plan A. I want Plans B through Z, too. No surprises."

"You know that's not how this works. I can't promise that there won't be surprises."

Slade shifts in the booth, clearly uncomfortable with Jackson's demands. I don't know Slade well, or at all for that matter, but his discomfort isn't because he's not confident in their ability. No, his discomfort is because Jackson is making this personal when that's the last thing it should be.

"No surprises or this is a no-go."

"I can't do that and you—"

"Fucking lie then!" Jackson shouts.

Slade's eyes go wide, and he glances at me quickly before nodding.

"No surprises."

19

JACKSON

"He's here."

Jett's eyes shift to me as he speaks to Mr. Vick. He seems more alert tonight than he usually does. I eye him warily, but I can't give him my full attention because of the woman on the stage. Katelyn is dancing her heart out, giving her best performance, and all I want to do is drag her out of here and do whatever it takes to make everything else disappear.

"He can join us here," Mr. Vick looks at Jett and dismisses him with a nod of his head. Jett goes to do his bidding.

"Sir, wouldn't it be better to do this in your office?" That is Plan A. The meeting taking place surrounded by customers is not even close to Plan B.

"Jack, thank you for your concern." He raises his tumbler up in mock salute. "I appreciate it, but I know what I'm doing."

I doubt that.

"Yes, sir."

Jett arrives at the table with Luciano, and a quick glance at Katelyn tells me she's noticed. Her steps falter for a split second, not long enough for anyone other than me to notice. Luciano sits down and Mr. Vick waves at me to stand and leave them to talk alone.

I have to hear what they say so I don't go too far. It helps that I planted a bug under the table earlier, before the club opened, and their conversation is also being played through one of the ear pieces I'm wearing. Fortunately, there are times I wear an earpiece as Vick's head of security, so it doesn't appear as if I'm doing anything different.

For the first half hour or so, the two men talk about nothing more than the weather and their families. I'm beginning to wonder if we'll ever get what we need for Slade and the others to move in.

"Saul, as much fun as this has been, I didn't invite you here to simply catch up." Mr. Vick's change in topic has my ears perking up. "Let's talk business."

"Of course," Luciano replies. "I trust that Jack told you my terms."

Mr. Vick narrows his eyes, almost imperceptibly, before he nods. "He did."

"Either you agree to them or you don't. It's that simple." Luciano shrugs as if they aren't discussing illegal activity.

"Business is never that simple. You know that." Mr. Vick thrusts his tumbler in the direction of Jett, indicating he wants a refill. "I have a counter proposal."

Come on you stupid fucks! Say something that I can use.

The song changes to something with so much bass that it becomes slightly more difficult to hear them. I glance at Katelyn, and she's still shaking her ass, a little less clothed than she was a few minutes ago. To the customers, she seems focused, like she's dancing just for them, but I know different. She's watching me like a hawk, her gaze only wavering when she glances toward the door.

After Jett hands Mr. Vick his refill, he steps up next to me.

He clasps his hands in front of him and seems to watch over the crowd, like he always does. Stoner is walking the floor, making sure that customers don't get out of control. Stoner may be crazy, but he's good at his job.

"I want in on whatever profit you make from my girls," Mr. Vick says.

"I'm sure you do, but—"

"You cut me in or you don't get access to them." Mr. Vick slams his glass down, whiskey sloshing over the side.

"Are you sure this is the hand you want to play?" Luciano asks, his voice deadly calm.

Mr. Vick stands up and flattens his hands on the table in front of him. "I'm not *playing* anything. This is the *only* card on the table."

Luciano stands and pulls his jacket off the back of his chair. He shrugs his arms through the sleeves, all the while staring down Mr. Vick. Recognizing that this might be our last chance, I press the button on my watch that will send the signal to Slade to raid this place.

"I'm not some pie-eyed girl you can jerk around and get to bend to your will." Luciano pivots to walk away but stops and glances over his shoulder. "No deal."

He walks away, but not toward the front door, like I'd expect. Before I can analyze what he's doing, all entrances to the club are flooded with FBI agents and SWAT. Mr. Vick looks at me and instead of panic, I see rage.

Chaos reigns down over the club. Customers scatter. Jett and Stoner act as buffers for our boss. I want to arrest his ass myself, but I can't. If this arrest doesn't stick, my cover needs to be maintained, so I help them. While we're trying to make it to the back door, I glance around the space, looking for Katelyn, but I don't see her.

Punches are thrown, bottles are broken, tables collapse.

Next thing I know, I'm tackled to the ground, air whooshing from me at the impact.

"Katelyn's fine." The voice in my ear is Slades. He's the one who tackled me.

Slade hauls me to my feet, and I make a show of resisting. Once he has the handcuffs in place, he stops and listens to whoever is on the other end of his earpiece. He nods at me. One slight movement of his head, and I know we're almost done. Mr. Vick has been arrested.

In order to keep up appearances, Slade reads me my rights as he drags me out of the club and shoves me into the waiting car.

Before he slams the door in my face, I ask, "Did we get Luciano?"

He shakes his head and then shuts the door. I wait there for what feels like hours before I'm transported to the station and booked. My cell isn't any less chaotic than The White Lily was. I have no idea where the others are. Mr. Vick, Stoner and Jett would have been put in a different cell so I could be released without them knowing. I have no idea where Katelyn is, but Slade said she was fine so I have to trust that.

I collapse on the dirty bench, beyond exhausted. The last year is catching up to me, but it's not quite over yet. I don't know how, but I manage to fall asleep until I hear my name being shouted.

"Mr. Duffy, wake up."

I look up and Slade's standing there, cup of coffee in hand and a giant smile on his face. I step through the gate when he opens it and take the caffeine he thrusts at me.

"Take me to Katelyn," I demand after taking a swig of the nasty brew.

"I am."

I follow Slade through the station, and when we reach an

interrogation room, he throws the door open, and I'm not sure what I'm seeing.

Katelyn is sitting at the table, her hands curled around a hot mug, and she's smiling. That's all well and good, but it's who she's smiling at that has me confused.

Across the table from her is Jett, and he's sporting a jacket that makes me question everything.

I read the bold block letters across the back.

DEA.

20

KATELYN

"I'm sorry for lying to you."

In the last hour, I've learned that telling a man 'don't worry about it' doesn't work when they're harboring a lot of guilt. I was stunned when Slade and Jett came into the room together. Even more surprising was learning that Jett is DEA and, just like Jackson, he's been undercover for quite a while, trying to nail Kevin Vick.

"Jett, let it go. Really, it's fine."

"It's not fine," Jackson snarls.

I glance at Jackson, and if I didn't know him, I'd probably be afraid of him. His jaw is clenched, his brown eyes reflect the light in such a way that makes them appear to be ringed in fire. It's scary, yet comforting.

"Well," I fold my hands on the table and lean forward. "Now what?"

"Now, it gets ugly." Jett smiles to soften the words, but it makes them no less worrisome.

"How so?" I need to know what to be prepared for.

"Kevin Vick is behind bars. Luciano is in the wind, and

while he wasn't my target, it's clear he's equally vile, if not more so. Jack and I—"

Jackson pounds the table with a fist. "It's Jackson."

"Right, sorry." Jett takes a deep breath. "Jackson and I need to spend some time comparing notes, reviewing the evidence we've managed to get while undercover, going over—"

"What would have happened if I hadn't walked in when I did?" Jackson's fury is verbally directed at Jett, but something seems off.

"Excuse me?"

"You heard me." Jackson stalks up to Jett and gets in his face. "If I hadn't *interrupted* the night you had Katelyn tied to that chair, what the fuck would you have done? Would you have stopped what was happening? Would you have sat back like a pussy and watched her suffer? Would you have helped to end her life? Huh? What the fuck would you have done?!"

"First of all," Jett stabs a finger into Jackson's chest, and I hear Slade mumble 'uh-oh' under his breath. "This isn't The White Lily and you don't get to order me around here. We're equals in this."

"The hell we—"

"Second," Jett continues as if Jackson hadn't spoken. "We've both done things we aren't proud of so don't go getting all holier than thou on me. You know as well as I do that being undercover means doing things we aren't proud of or that we wouldn't do under normal circumstances. Banging waitresses ring a bell?"

Seconds tick by and just when I think Jackson's going to let that comment slide, he draws his arm back and lands a blow to Jett's face that has his head whipping to the side. I sit there, frozen in the chair, time seeming to stand still. Slade rushes to haul Jackson back and shoves him down into a chair. Jackson resists but not for long.

Jett swipes at the blood dribbling from the cut on his cheek. His chest is heaving, and for a minute, he looks like he's going to launch himself at Jackson and pummel him. Instead, he controls his breathing and lets out a chuckle.

"Feel better?" He flips a chair around and straddles it, never taking his eyes off of Jackson. When Jackson doesn't answer, Jett continues. "Look, I get that you're pissed. I would be too, but this isn't about us. We need to find a way to work together."

"He's right, Jackson." Slade sits down next to me and leans back in his chair.

"Whose side are you on?" Jackson glares at Slade.

"Same side as you. Same side as Jett. I'm on the side that ensures Kevin Vick stays put."

Jackson stares at Slade, as if weighing his words to determine if they're true or not. When Slade doesn't relent, Jackson shifts his focus to Jett and then to me. For a moment, I forget that he's supposed to be this big bad FBI guy. I forget that he's strong and loyal and protective.

I forget because when he's looking at me, he lets his guard down, just a little bit. He looks at me and all I see is pain mixed with guilt. I lean across the table and put my hands out, palms up. He stares at them for a split second before putting his hands on mine and when we touch, the rest of the room fades, disappears until it's just him and me.

"I'm not them," I say.

"I know."

"You're not who?"

Slade and Jett speak at the same time, reminding me that Jackson and I aren't alone. I squeeze Jackson's hand. He hangs on to me a minute longer before letting go and leaning back in his chair. He folds his arms across his chest, closing himself off to the conversation. I hold his gaze and he nods, almost imperceptibly, giving me permission to explain.

"His wife and son," I answer the question.

"You're married?" Jett's head whips around to pin Jackson with his glare.

"They're dead." Jackson's response is sharp, his tone hollow.

"Shit." Jett looks at me and then Slade. I can tell the second things start falling into place for him because his body stiffens and his eyes widen. "Vick killed them." It isn't a question.

"Not personally, no." Jackson drops his arms and takes a deep breath. "But he's responsible even if he didn't pull the trigger."

"I'm sorry, man. I didn't know."

"Forget it." Jackson shoves to his feet and starts to pace.

"Okay." Jett heaves a sigh. "Why don't we continue this discussion tomorrow? We're not going to get anything accomplished tonight and besides, Vick is in a cell."

"Works for me." With that, Jackson throws open the door and slams it behind him.

Jett and Slade stare at the closed door before shifting their attention to me. I'm too stunned to speak. I figured I'd be going home with Jackson but apparently not. I paste a smile on my face and rise from my chair.

"Um, can someone take me home? Please?" I hold my breath and pray that it's Slade and not Jett that offers. I know Jett's one of the good guys, but despite my earlier don't-worry-about-it attitude, I'm not quite ready to be alone with him.

"I can take you." Slade smiles. "Let me just check on him first and then we can leave."

"Thanks."

"Don't mention it."

When Slade exits the room, I'm in exactly the position I

was hoping to avoid. Alone with Jett. He clears his throat and it startles me.

"I guess I'll see you tomorrow."

I nod. He stares at me a second longer before turning and walking out the door. I slump back into my chair, and my body deflates. I'm exhausted. Physically, mentally, emotionally. I want Jackson to come back in here and tell me it will all be okay. Maybe he will.

When the door swings open, my heart flutters, thinking it's him. I glance up and Slade is filling the doorway. My hopes are dashed, and it takes everything in me not to give in to the disappointment.

"Ready?"

"Is he okay?" I can't leave until I know he's going to be okay.

"Yeah." Slade shoves his fingers through his hair. "He will be."

∾

I flip the lock and lean my forehead against the door. Slade checked out my apartment, made sure it was safe, before he left. I wasn't worried, but he said that it was better to be safe than sorry.

I trudge to the bathroom, intent on taking a shower and washing Kitty Kat and jail off of me. I always take a shower after a shift, scrubbing almost to the point of pain, and tonight is no exception. I toss my clothes to the floor and step under the lukewarm spray.

When I can't possibly get any cleaner, I get out, wrapping myself up in a towel. I stare at my reflection in the mirror, and tentatively touch the cut on my lip. It's healing better than I thought it would, thanks to Jackson's attention to it the night it happened. At the thought of him, my chest constricts and it becomes hard to breathe.

How did he become so important to me so quickly? I want to see him, feel him, love him. I want to make him forget his tragic past, even if only for a little while.

A knock on my door startles me from my thoughts. As the knock intensifies, so does my fear. It's way too early for it to be anything good, and the pounding is way too intense to be anyone I'd want to see. I scramble to the living room, remembering the cell phone that Jackson gave me in case of an emergency. Someone banging on my door so hard they're going to break it down qualifies.

Just as I reach into my bag and wrap my fingers around the device, it vibrates. My heart is beating out of my chest. I glance at the text notification and sag to the floor when I read the words.

It's Jackson. Open the door.

Relief battles fury. I'm glad he's here, but damn, he scared the hell out of me. Why didn't he just call out to me when he knocked, let me know it was him? With that thought in mind, I get to my feet and take the few steps to the door. I disengage the lock and throw it open, intent on giving him a piece of my mind.

All of my anger dissipates when I see him, forearms braced against the doorframe, head hanging down. I step to the side and wait for him to enter. When he does, he turns, locks the door, and leans against it for support, much like I did after Slade left. I step up behind him and wrap my arms around his waist. He takes the comfort I'm offering, and we stand there like that for a few minutes.

When he straightens, I drop my arms and step back, allowing

him to turn around and face me. His eyes are darker than normal and remind me of chocolate as he takes in my towel-clad body. His nostrils flare. His throat bobs as he swallows, and his biceps twitch as he clenches and unclenches his hands.

"You should tell me to leave."

My throat is dry, making words impossible, so I settle on shaking my head.

"I'm not good for you right now."

He takes a step toward me, and I take a step back, resecuring my towel. The reaction is involuntary and I mentally chastise myself for it. He takes another step, and I force my feet to remain in place. His stare is simultaneously scary as hell and an aphrodisiac of monumental proportions.

"I'm more like Jack than you deserve."

He reaches out and wraps his fingers around my hair, tugging me forward. His grip tightens and my scalp stings. I don't stop him though. I'm not sure I even could.

"I know you said we had to wait, but I can't," he growls. His free hand yanks the towel from my body and tosses it to the floor. "I need to bury myself inside of you."

Jackson bends and sucks a nipple between his lips, his teeth grazing the sensitive peak. My head falls back, and my knees grow weak. He grabs my ass, lifting and turning me in one swift move, slamming me against the wall. My legs wrap around his hips, the denim he's wearing infuriating. He raises my hands above my head and pins them beneath his, holding me hostage in the most delicious of ways.

"Jackson…"

"Yeah, darlin'?"

He switches to the other nipple, and I forget what I wanted to say. My hips undulate, trying to find that friction that will take me over the edge. His mouth moves to mine, and the kiss is deep, fueled by emotion so intense it should be scary.

Without letting me fall, he leaves the support of the wall and carries me to the couch, dropping me to the cushions. When I reach for his clothes he shoves my hands away and strips himself. When he's as naked as I am, he makes no move to join me. He stands there, staring at me, his chest heaving and muscles bunching.

His hard cock juts from his body, like a beacon. I push myself up onto my elbows, bringing my head to the perfect height. I hesitate, sure he's going to stop me, but instead, he bends to push me back down and straddles my face. His balls hit my chin and I grip his dick to line it up with my lips.

Jackson sucks in a breath when my tongue swirls around his mushroomed tip, tasting him. He braces his left hand on the arm of the couch, and his right hand grips the back of my head and pulls me forward, forcing my jaw to widen and accommodate his size. I seal my lips around his cock and hum as he fucks my mouth.

I cup his balls with one hand and reach down to tease my clit with the other. Jackson reaches between us and pulls my hand back up, refusing to allow me any pleasure beyond what I get from sucking him off. I'm wet, needy, frustrated.

Jackson increases his thrusts, and each time he bumps the back of my throat, I swallow, knowing that only intensifies the experience for him. When his body stiffens and he tries to pull away, I dig my nails into his ass and hold him to me.

"Fuuuuck!" He shouts out his orgasm, and I suck and swallow until he softens on my tongue.

His arms are shaking, and I'm sure he's spent. I need to come, so I once again reach for my clit only to have him stop me. I look into his eyes, silently pleading for him to let me find release. He breaks the stare and scoots backward on his knees, pulling me along with him, until he's off the opposite end of the couch. He stands there, looking down at me with hunger in his eyes. I drop my gaze and see that he's hard again, ready for more.

He wraps his hands behind my knees and tugs me until my ass is on the arm of the couch, spreading my legs until my pussy is on display. A grin tugs at the corners of his lips as he bends to his knees and touches his tongue to my inner thigh. He traces a fiery path up until he reaches my sweet spot.

I buck my hips at the contact and cry out. I try to clamp my legs together, not because I don't want what he's doing but because it's so intense I'm not sure I can handle it. He holds my knees apart and assaults my clit, sucking, licking, nipping. I cry out, sure I'm going to explode, and he pulls away, letting me settle. While my breathing evens out, he lets go of one knee and teases my folds.

"You're glistening."

He penetrates me with a thick digit, finger fucking me before adding another and then a third. He curls his fingers, hitting my g-spot, but I need more. He puts pressure on my clit with his thumb and I shout.

"Ah, that's what you need."

He continues to fuck me wtih his hand and leans forward, replacing his thumb with his flattened tongue. My head thrashes from side to side as he works his magic. My legs shake, my body quivers. Jackson doesn't let up until my walls contract around his fingers, sucking them deeper, and my orgasm makes me spasm out of control.

I'm not even halfway back to Earth when he pulls me toward him by my knees and impales me in one smooth stroke. My back slides against the rough couch fibers, and I know I'm gonna be sore but I don't care. He fills me up to the point of having no room for anything but the most basic of desires.

As he fucks me, his face is twisted in pleasure and I can't help but stare. His hips are flying and in my position, I can't meet his thrusts but I don't need to. This is about him, about what he needs. He's using me and I want him to. I want to give him a place to release all of his demons so I can take away his pain, keep it inside of me where it can't touch him.

His thrusts continue, even as his body tenses. I reach down and circle my clit so we can come together. We both explode and the intensity of it is almost too much. His body goes limp, but he doesn't move, doesn't speak. As he slides out of me, he runs his fingertips over my legs, raising goosebumps.

Jackson remains silent as he steps to the side of the couch and scoops me up in his arms. He places a kiss on my lips, the contact sweet, brief, and then carries me to my bedroom. He lays me on the bed and crawls in beside me, pulling the covers over us. I roll to my side and reach back to pull his arm around me.

He buries his face in my hair, and I swear I can feel his heartbeat thumping against my back. We lay there, no sound other than our breathing, and he throws a leg over mine, holding me hostage. I imagine he thinks he scared me but he didn't. I'm not going anywhere.

"Get some sleep," I whisper.

Jackson takes a deep breath, and when I don't feel his chest move, I know he's holding it. When he blows the breath out, it's like he's breathing out every awful thing that's ever happened to him.

"She was gonna leave me."

"What?" I try to turn over so I can face him, but he holds me in place.

"My wife. Melinda." His arm tightens around me. "We fought that last night. She was angry that I re-upped. I was scheduled to deploy, and the night before I left, we argued."

"I'm so sorry, Jackson."

"She told me that she and Ben might not be there when I got back." His breath hitches. "I never thought…"

"It's not your fault." I forcefully turn around, not letting him stop me, and place my hands on his cheeks. "You couldn't have known."

"I left them." His eyes are bright with unshed tears. "I was supposed to protect them, and instead I left them and they were murdered." He squeezes his eyes shut, and a tear slips down his cheek, hitting my finger. "They were shot for a quick high and whatever cash they could get their hands on. How fucked up is that?"

I kiss him, letting my lips linger. After a few seconds of contact, the dam breaks. His body shakes with sobs so I pull him to me and let him cry. He mumbles every few seconds, and I whisper assurances until he finally calms. He pulls away from me and looks into my eyes.

"I'm sorry."

"For what?" I ask. "You're allowed to break down, Jackson. You lost your family."

"It's just…"

"What?"

"If I hadn't left, they'd still be alive. My *son* would still be alive."

"Don't." I shake my head. "Don't live your life on what-ifs. That's no way to live."

"Maybe not, but it's all I've got."

"You sure about that?"

He looks at me and his eyes narrow. "What do you mean?"

I shrug, not sure how to answer him. He has me, whether either of us are prepared to admit that. I may not be *her*, but she's his past. I can be his future.

"Let's get some sleep." He brushes hair off my cheek and

smiles, but it doesn't reach his eyes. "It's been a long night and we're gonna have a lot to do later."

"Okay."

I roll over and scoot my ass toward him so he can hold me as we lie there. I stare at the wall for a long time, waiting for his breathing to even out, waiting for him to sleep. When his body finally relaxes, my heart cracks and I struggle to hold in the tears. Tears for Jackson, the husband who was made a widower, the father who was robbed of his son, for the man hell bent on avenging those he's lost. My tears are also for me, the woman who wants to make it better but who has no clue how to compete with a ghost.

21

JACKSON

"*At ease, soldier.*"

My commanding officer entered my tent, and I automatically stood at attention. That's what they taught us. It was drilled into us until it became reflex. I relax my stance.

"Sir?"

"We just received a call from the States." Runyon is as serious as they come, a force to be reckoned with, but right here, right now, in front of me, he's different. "Why don't you sit down?" He nods toward my cot.

I do as he suggests, and he sits next to me. This can't be good.

"I'm sorry to have to tell you this, son, but," he takes a deep breath, blows it out. "Mel and Benny..."

I shoot up and whirl on him. "What? What about them?"

"Jackson, they were killed."

I shake my head, put my hands over my ears. "No. No no no no."

"I'm so sorry, son."

"No no no no."

My knees buckle, and Runyon is there, catching me as I collapse, holding me as I lose my shit. I want to ask questions. I *know I should ask questions. But right now, I can't breathe, let alone speak.*

I toss and turn as sweat beads on my forehead in my sleep, and the images shift.

"Ashes to ashes, dust to dust..."

The preacher's words fade away as I stare at the two caskets in front of me, suspended above two six-foot deep holes in the dirt. I don't want to be here. I shouldn't be here. They shouldn't be here.

Benny, my innocent little boy, never even had a chance to crawl, to walk, to live and love. And Melinda, my incredible wife, protected him until her last breath. The police told me that when they arrived at the scene, Melinda was holding our son in her arms, as if trying to shield him, protect him. Unfortunately, she wasn't bullet-proof. Both of them died instantly, the bullet tearing through Mel and hitting Benny in the chest.

"Jackson."

I raise my head to look at the preacher.

"We're going to close the caskets now. Do you want to see them one last time?"

I'd opted for a graveside funeral. Benny deserved to enjoy the outdoors, to feel the sun on his face. And Melinda loved nature. We weren't church people so having it at a chapel or whatever had been out of the question.

I nod to the preacher and stand on shaky legs. I look at Benny first. He looks like he's sleeping. They did an incredible job of covering his wound. I huff out a breath. It is more than a wound. It's a kill shot. I lean in and kiss my boy's head.

I move to Melinda's coffin. Anger surges through me, but I force it down. Had she somehow known this would happen? She'd told me they might not be there when I got back. No. No, this is not what she meant.

As I'm staring at her face, memorizing every detail, it changes, morphs into someone else. I don't recognize the woman at first. I whirl around and everyone is gone. My friends, my family, they're all gone except for one man sitting in the only chair that remains.

"Jackson, I don't know what to say," *the man looks sad, and it takes me a minute to place him.*

"Slade? What are you doing here? You're not supposed to be here."

"I couldn't stay away. Not for this." *He nods toward the casket that's now behind me.*

"But you didn't even know them." *I shake my head. I'm so confused.*

"Katelyn didn't deserve this, man."

My heart seizes and for a second, I think I'm going to die. "What are you talking about?"

"It's your fault, Jackson. You know that, right? Katelyn is dead because of you."

"But... no." *I don't want to turn around, but it's like I have no control over my body, like I'm floating and some invisible force is tugging the strings.*

When my gaze lands on the woman again, it hits me. This is Katelyn. And according to Slade, I'm responsible for her death.

I throw myself on the casket and let out a scream.

"Jackson!"

That's not right. How is she talking when she's dead?

"Jackson, you need to wake up." Someone is shaking me, but who? "It's just a dream. Wake up!"

I bolt upright and try to suck in air. The screaming is still echoing in my head. I shake off the hand on my arm and throw the covers to the side so I can get up. I need to get to Katelyn. I need to warn her. Of what, I have no idea.

"Jackson, where are you going?"

"I need to save her," I shout and spin around to face... Katelyn. My body goes limp, and I collapse to the floor.

"Jackson." She rushes to my side and brushes my hair out

of my eyes. I'm slick with sweat and no doubt stink, but she makes no move to pull away.

"I thought…" I gulp. "In my dream, you were dead."

"I'm right here. I'm alive."

She grips my hand and brings it to her chest, splaying it over her heart. I feel the thump of her heartbeat, and while it's a little fast, it's there. She's alive. She's not dead. I didn't get her killed.

"C'mon." She tries to stand and tug me up with her. I'm not much help, but when we're both on our feet, she urges me back toward the bed where we both sit. "Wanna talk about it?"

I shake my head. Fuck no I don't want to talk about it. My nightmares have been bad enough since Runyon came into my tent. I didn't think it was possible for them to get worse. I'd been wrong.

"Okay."

"What time is it?" I ask.

Katelyn leans across me and pulls her cell phone off the nightstand and glances at it.

"Little after noon."

"We're gonna need to—"

My own cell rings from the other room. I rush out there to grab it and have to force myself to remain calm when I see that it's Slade. He doesn't know it, but he just accused me of getting Katelyn killed. It may have been a nightmare, but it felt very real.

"What's up?"

"Vick was released." Slade's words slam into me.

Katelyn walks into the room just as I fall back onto the couch. She rushes to my side but halts when she sees my face.

"How the fuck is that possible?" I bark into the phone.

"Because people don't know how to do their goddamn

jobs." Slade's tone is as angry as mine, and I hear glass shatter on his end.

"What's that supposed to mean?"

"I don't have all of the specifics yet, but his lawyer got him out on a technicality." Slade lets out a hollow laugh. "A goddamn technicality. You need to get to the club. Jett's already there."

"Yeah, okay." I thrust my fingers through my hair.

"Do you want me to call Katelyn and let her know?"

"Nah, I'll tell her."

"Tell me what?" Katelyn asks.

"Gotta say, man, I thought it would've taken you a little longer to come around." Slade's chuckle is annoying.

"Fuck off," I snap.

"Whatever. I'll let you go. Check in later."

The line goes dead. I pull the phone away from my ear and stare at the screen, trying to come up with a way to tell Katelyn that this isn't over yet.

"Jackson, what do you need to tell me?"

I hate the worry in her voice, and I know that I'm only going to make it worse. But I can't lie to her. Not only does she know there's something that needs to be told, but I promised her no secrets. Stupid fucking promise.

"Darlin'," I pause and take a deep breath. "Vick was released."

"How?" She stands and starts to pace. "I mean, you got him. He did whatever you needed him to do to be arrested. He can't be released."

I stand and go to her, wrap my arms around her. If I'm worried, she's gotta be fucking terrified.

"We'll get him again." I kiss the top of her head, breathe in her scent. "We'll get him."

"We already got him!" she yells while she tries to pummel my chest with her clenched fists.

"I know."

"We already got him," she repeats as her assault dies down.

"I know."

"Now what?" she mumbles.

"We head to the club and take things as they come." I pull her away from me and look into her eyes. "We'll figure out another way."

"What about Luciano? He got away. What about Brandie?"

"We'll figure out another way."

The truth is, I have no idea how we're going to nail Luciano and save Brandie. All I know is I'll move heaven and earth for this woman. I'll protect her. I'll get my revenge. I'll save her friend.

Those are my only options.

22

MR. VICK

"Sir?"

There are no windows in my office. I specifically chose this office because of that fact. My business doesn't need to be conducted in a damn fishbowl, however, after being cooped up in a cell for hours, I want a fucking window.

"Sir?"

I slowly spin my chair around and glare at Jett. He picked me up from the station after my attorney got me out on a technicality. At the time, I thought it was suspicious that he'd gotten there so fast, but he assured me that he had never left because he knew I'd get out and need a ride. I'm not sure if I believe that, but at this point, what choice do I have?

"Explain to me again why you're out and Stoner isn't."

"He punched that cop during booking, sir. Remember? Broke the fucker's nose."

Ah, yes. Stoner lost his shit and managed to get himself in an even deeper pile of the stuff. He knows better than to get violent with the law, or any other time than when instructed by me for that matter, but he cracked.

"And Jack?" I have yet to speak to my head of security, but Jett told me he'd been released, as well.

"On his way, according to the last text."

I glance at my watch, the Rolex now sporting a fresh crack on the face of it because of some asshole who doesn't know how to do his damn job and secure evidence. I look back to Jett.

"We open in an hour. Are all the girls here?"

"All except for Kitty Kat."

"Kitty Kat's here, boss." Jack strolls through the door with his hands in his pockets and a smug smile on his face. "Just dropped her off at the dressing room."

"Good." I rise from my chair and step around my desk. "Shut the door."

Jack does as instructed and returns to his place in front of me, next to Jett. Both are looking at me expectantly. I take a minute to compose my words.

"Last night was—"

"A cluster-fuck." Jack scowls and crosses his arms over his chest.

"A set-up," I finish. "That's the only thing that makes sense. Luciano was here and surprise, surprise, the bastard got away."

"You think he had something to do with the raid?" Jett's eyebrows raise in question.

"I know he did." I just can't prove it. Not yet. "Jack, I want you to set up another meeting with him. Neutral territory this time. I don't want him in my club."

"Sir, are you sure that's the best—"

"You'll do as you're told," I snap.

"And if he refuses?"

"He won't." The plan in my head is taking shape, and I smile for the first time since walking out of the police station.

"You know this how?" Jett asks.

"I'm gonna make it worth his while."

"How?"

"By sweetening the deal." Tingles dance down my spine as excitement builds. "We're going to give him what he originally asked for and then some."

"I'm not sure I'm following." Jack looks at Jett, who only shrugs. There's a reason I run this enterprise and they don't. They're too stupid to think outside the box.

"Sit down." I nod toward the chairs, and when they sit, I do the same. "Luciano is as predictable as death and taxes. He likes what he likes and that's never going to change. Jack," I focus my stare on him. "The man thrives on money and hoes. He's still going to get the money he wants, but he's also going to get Kitty Kat and three other hand picked girls."

"Sir, are you sure about this? Luciano wasn't too keen on Kitty Kat after meeting her. Said she'd be too much work to break."

"So break her for him," I demand. "And fast. I want this meeting to happen soon."

"And the other girls? Which strippers do you want to give him?"

"Just Kitty Kat. Get the others off the street." I wave my hand dismissively. "You pick. Just make sure that they're young and no one will miss them when they're gone."

"Yes, sir." Jett and Jack speak simultaneously.

I wish Stoner was here. This is the first time I'm really bringing them in on the other aspects of my business, and I'm not sure how they'll do. Stoner, though. That fuck is crazy and wouldn't bat an eye.

"You're dismissed. Go and do whatever it is you have to do to make this all happen."

After they're both gone, I open my desk drawer and pull

out a baggie. I toss it on the surface and stare at it for a moment before opening it and emptying it's contents on top of strewn papers.

It's been a stressful twenty-four hours and I need to unwind a bit.

23

KATELYN

"Are you going to eat that?"

When I shake my head, Jackson stabs the steak in front of me with his fork, transferring it to his own plate. I stare at him while he eats his dinner, and what's left of mine. Normally, I'd be chowing down with him, but not tonight. Tonight is different.

"It's going to be okay."

Jackson reaches across the table and covers my hand with his. His gaze never wavers. I don't know what he sees when he looks at me, but if it's anything resembling what I'm feeling inside, it's not pretty.

It's been a month since we were 'arrested' and nothing has happened. No movement on the case, no contact from Luciano, nothing. Until yesterday. One text and my faux idyllic life is crumbling.

"Katelyn, you need to try to eat something." Jackson gets up from the table and clears the dishes.

"I'm not hungry."

"I don't care." He stomps back to the table and pulls me up

from my chair, turning me to face him. "I don't give a damn if you don't want to eat. You need to."

"Don't yell at me!"

My shout is punctuated by pounding on the door. Jackson glares at me for a moment before letting my arms go and stalking to answer it. I can see him from where I'm standing, and when he swings the door open, Jett and Slade enter.

The three of them settle in the living room while I'm rooted to the same spot. I listen to them talk about anything and everything but what they need to be talking about. When I can't take it any longer, I force my feet to move until I'm standing in front of them, the coffee table separating us.

They stop talking and stare at me, as if I'm a specimen they can put under a microscope to inspect. None of them say a word. I glare back, not wanting to be the weak one, the one to break eye contact.

"What's the plan?" I ask, breaking the silence.

Slade huffs out a breath and stands. "We've been over the plan at least a dozen times since yesterday. Do we really need to go over it again?"

"Yes," I snap.

"Fine." Jackson stands, too. "We go to work like any other night. You go on stage like you always do. Stoner will be there like he always is. I know you don't like him, but it's his job and we need to keep things as normal as we can. Jett and I are going to take Mr. Vick to the meeting with Luciano. Slade will be in the vicinity, listening to the conversation. We'll get them to say something, anything, to incriminate themselves. Slade and his team will swoop in and arrest them."

"That's an oversimplified plan, don't you think?" I rest my hands on my hips, frustrated by their ability to make this seem like it's not a huge deal. Like tonight isn't the night to end all nights.

"I know it seems like it," Jett says as he, too, stands. "And yeah, to a degree, you're right. But it's all we've got."

"I don't like it. I want to go to the meeting." I've begged and pleaded to be a part of the meeting between Luciano and Mr. Vick. The answer has remained the same.

"No," Jackson grits out.

"But what if Brandie's there? She's gonna need me." My eyes burn and I know I'm close to losing it.

"If she's there, we'll get her out." This has been Slade's stock response whenever I bring up Brandie.

"It just makes no sense to me. Why tonight? It's been a month!" I shake my head, try to reign in my emotions. "And why does it have to be at Luciano's place? I thought it was supposed to take place on neutral territory."

"It was, but Luciano insisted. It's the meeting we need, so does the why and where really matter?" Jackson takes a few steps toward me and cups my cheeks. "Darlin', it's happening. And it's going to be fine."

He doesn't sound convinced, but what choice do I have but to believe him? To trust him? He hasn't let me down yet.

"If you say so," I mumble and step out of his embrace. "I'm going to get ready."

I leave the three of them in the living room and go take a shower. My nerves are beyond shot and maybe, just maybe, the hot water and alone time will help calm them. As I wash my hair, I review the plan in my head. I'd feel better about this whole thing if Jackson was going to be the one looking out for me.

The longer I think, the more stressed I feel. Maybe alone time wasn't a good thing. As I'm getting out of the shower my stomach does somersaults and I drop to my knees in front of the toilet. I haven't eaten all day, so I dry heave until I can't dry heave any longer.

I brace my hands on the toilet seat and hoist myself up. I glance at the mirror and wince at the pale reflection staring back at me. I finish getting ready and apply a generous amount of make-up. No sense in worrying Jackson more than he already is. Besides, I'm not sick, just scared.

The ride to the club is silent, other than the pounding of my heart. When we arrive, Jackson and I enter together and before we part ways, he pulls me toward him and wraps his arms around me. I melt into him, soaking up everything he has to give.

"It'll all be over after tonight," he mumbles into my hair.

My throat is clogged with emotion, making it impossible to speak, so I nod. So many things can go wrong and I've thought of all of them.

"Tomorrow, we'll talk about where we go from here."

Again, I nod. We've spent every possible minute together over the last month, and while it's been amazing, there's always been this investigation hanging over us. I'm excited to see what happens next and simultaneously terrified that I won't get to find out.

Jackson urges me away from him and frames my face. He leans down and kisses me, pouring everything into the moment. When he turns and walks away, I stare at his back. Just before he turns the corner, I call out to him, unable to let him go.

"Jackson!"

"Yeah?" He glances over his shoulder at me.

"I, uh…I'm… " My brain shuts down, and I fidget with my hands. This isn't the time or place so I shake my head. "Nothing. Good luck."

He smiles at me and I memorize it, memorize him. Then

he's gone and I'm left to get dressed just to get naked. I head toward the dressing room, and when I enter, I'm surprised to see it empty. Usually a few other girls are here by now getting ready. Especially since they all go on before me.

I sit on the stool at my station and stare at my reflection. The make-up I applied at home helped tremendously, but I need to work on a touch-up because the unforgiving lights on the stage will out me.

"Kitty Kat, you ready for tonight?" Sapphire struts toward me with a smile on her face and her bag slung over her shoulder.

"I guess." I frown, unsure of what she's referring to. "Just a normal night."

"Are you sure about that?" she asks as she drops her bag to the floor. She's still smiling, but there's nothing friendly in her expression.

"I, uh, yes?" I don't sound sure. Not even a little bit.

"Ya know, I've been here a long time. Worked my way up the stripper pole, so to speak." She laughs at her own joke. "I was the best. The girl every customer wanted."

"Where are you going with this, Saph?" I turn around so I can face her and not our reflections in the mirror. "What's your point?"

"I ran the stage. I had everything a girl could ask for. Good job, adoring fans, a sugar daddy and a man who understood what I craved. I had it all." Saphire's eyes narrow and the smile disappears. "And then you came along."

"Get over yourself." I huff out a breath. I don't have time for her petty jealousy tonight.

"Yeah, see, that's the thing. I don't want to."

She reaches out and grabs my arm. I struggle against her hold, but she's stronger than she looks. I catch a glimpse of the syringe in her other hand a split second before something stings my neck.

"And now I don't have to."

Her hollow laugh is the last thing I hear before my world goes black.

24

JACKSON

Trust your gut, son. It's what made you a good soldier, and it will make you a damn fine cop.

As we sit here, waiting for Luciano to arrive, my old commanding officer's voice plays on a loop in my head. Right now, my gut is screaming that something is wrong. Problem is, I can't simply act on that without raising some red flags for Mr. Vick.

"Wasn't he supposed to be here by now?"

Speaking of Mr. Vick, he's getting impatient, and I can't say that I blame him. Luciano is an asshole and hasn't made it to where he is without capitalizing on that trait from time to time.

"Yeah, he was." Jett is just as frustrated as I am.

We both need for this to end. Tonight. Our two agencies have come to an agreement that Vick will be prosecuted by the DEA and Luciano, the FBI. I hate that solution, but it makes sense. Jett and Slade know I want revenge on Vick, so I'm hoping they stick to the plan of allowing me a few uninterrupted minutes alone with him.

STARK REVENGE

"Are you sure you got the address right?"

I glance at Vick in the rearview mirror. He knows I've met with Luciano before, but he has no idea that it was here, at the warehouse.

I've got the address you dumb motherfucker.

"I'm sure." I make a show of double checking my phone for the details and turn the screen for him to see. "Right place, right time. Luciano just wants to make you sweat."

As I slide my cell back into my pocket, I picture Luciano in his underground mansion watching us via security monitors and getting a kick out of the fact that we're just sitting here. Not for the first time, I wonder if Mr. Vick got the details wrong and we're supposed to actually go inside rather than wait out here in the dark.

Another twenty minutes pass before a vehicle pulls into the parking lot. I have to chuckle because it's just like in the movies. We're in a black sedan with tinted windows and an almost identical vehicle is what is pulling in. The other sedan parks and all passengers of both vehicles exit and converge on the door to enter the building.

"Thank you for coming," Luciano says as Jimmy, the goon from my last visit, unlocks the door to the warehouse.

"You gave me little choice," Mr. Vick snaps.

Jett and I exchange glances over Mr. Vick's head. He's pissed that he was kept waiting which only serves to make this situation more dangerous. Mr. Vick is a smart man but anger him and he's a loose cannon.

The five of us walk through the warehouse, toward the stairs that lead to Luciano's private quarters and the closer we get, the lower my stomach drops. If we go down there, we'll be unarmed and potentially ambushed because I know that Luciano doesn't necessarily make his people follow the rules.

When we reach the locker, Luciano instructs us to leave our weapons and cell phones inside, same as before. I hesitate, as do Mr. Vick and Jett.

"Jack, Jack, Jack," Luciano quips. "You know the drill. I suggest you do as you're told and instruct your boss and the other ape to do the same."

I know Jett and I won't be able to get what we need if we stay here, at an impasse, so I nod at the two men with me and we all deposit our guns and electronic devices in the locker. What they don't know is my watch has a mic on it so Slade is still able to hear what's going on and there's a button that I can push if we need back-up.

Like a lamb to slaughter, we follow Luciano down the steps, and when he allows us entry into his 'foyer', Mr. Vick and Jett gasp at the sight. It seems they're just as surprised as I was the first time around.

"This is quite impressive." Mr. Vick's tone is a mixture of awe and condescension.

I can see the wheels turning in his head, trying to calculate what it would take for him to have a place like this. Unfortunately for him, he'll never find out because his only concern with regards to his future will be whether or not he lets other inmates make him the cellblock bitch.

"I'm glad you like it."

Luciano walks to the center of the space and steps on the almost hidden button, causing the phone to rise out of the floor. Much like before, he calls someone, but this time he doesn't instruct them to meet us in the library. He asks them if the east wing is prepared, and apparently satisfied with the answer, he hangs up.

"I don't usually allow people to see my business up-close, but I'm making an exception because I think we can be mutually beneficial for one another."

"I'm quite clear on how you think my business can benefit you, but I've yet to be convinced as to how you can benefit my business." Mr. Vick is afraid of this guy, yet he continues to push his buttons.

"Follow me."

Luciano walks away, not bothering to see if we follow because he knows we will. We have no choice. Everything we pass screams money from the wall decorations to the displays of antiques to the marble floor. When Mr. Vick and Luciano are several feet ahead of us, Jett smacks my arm.

"This is some next level shit," Jett whispers.

"It's fucked up is what it is."

When we come to a door, Luciano enters a code and the door swings open. What's beyond that barrier is much different than anything we've seen so far, and that sense of dread that started in the parking lot intensifies.

The floor is no longer marble and the decor no longer gives off an expensive vibe. The east wing, as Luciano called it, resembles a hospital more than a home. The furnishings are not what worry me though. It's the smell that seems to ooze from the walls that has me cringing.

"What the fuck is that stench?" Mr. Vick asks as he covers his nose and mouth with his hand.

"That is the smell of money," Luciano says proudly, with a shit-eating grin on his face.

He walks down the corridor and stops at a room. The door is steel and has a small window with bars and no glass. He motions for us to take a peek inside. Mr. Vick eyes him suspiciously before he steps up to the window. He has to stand on his tip-toes to see anything, but when he does, he drops his arm and a laugh escapes him.

"I see you've made use of your payment." Mr. Vick turns back around to grin at Luciano.

"I have indeed." Luciano shifts his attention to me. "Take a look, Jack. I think you'll like what you see."

I'm going to hate what I see, but I do as he says, forcing myself to temper any reaction to what's inside the room. My dinner threatens to make an appearance as I peer through the bars. Brandie is lying naked on a linoleum floor. It appears to have been white with black speckles at one point, but now it's stained crimson. There's a drain in the center of the room and shackles attached to the wall. A chain connects Brandie to those shackles by her ankle, and she's also hooked up to an IV stand.

Why the fuck would he think I would like this?

Because you're Jack Duffy and the last time you were here you talked about how you could 'break' women.

I take a deep breath and return my attention to the men behind me. Mr. Vick is still grinning, and Luciano appears to be anxiously awaiting my reaction.

"Looks like she may have gotten a little out of hand."

"Ah, yes. She was quite difficult after your last visit. Had to go back to the basics with her, but she's coming around. She'll be obedient once again."

The evil with which it takes a man to discuss a woman like a puppy in training is staggering. A year ago I thought I'd be avenging my family and taking down a drug operation, not having to pretend that human trafficking is something I condone.

"I take it there are more?" Mr. Vick asks, motioning down the hall to the other doors that are visible.

"There are." Luciano's grin turns even more sinister. "There's one in particular that I think you're going to like."

He walks to the end of the hall, and as we pass each door, I notice plaques that read 'Phase 1', 'Phase 2', 'Phase 3', 'Punishment', and 'Ready for Release'. This operation is much more organized and established than I could have imagined.

When Luciano stops at the last door on the left, I read its plaque: 'Newly Acquired'. I know that just seeing the east wing is enough to make an arrest, but only of Luciano. If both Jett and I want to close our cases, we need more. Which means I'm going to have to look into another room and listen to these pieces of shit discuss *business.*

Mr. Vick steps up to the window, and his posture goes rigid. He spins around and glares at Luciano.

"What's the meaning of this?"

I glance at Jett, who's been silent this entire time. He hasn't seen what's behind the doors. but at Mr. Vick's outburst, he decides to look.

"Jesus," he whispers as he turns around and looks at me with wide eyes.

He's a DEA agent, but the look on his face tells me he's never before seen anything like what he just laid eyes on. He tips his head toward the window, indicating that I should look. I know by his reaction that I'm not going to like what I see, so I mentally brace myself.

When I step up to the door, I close my eyes, stalling as long as possible.

"Open your fucking eyes!" Luciano demands from behind me.

I inhale and hold my breath as I follow his command. Air rushes past my lips as my blood begins to boil. The room is identical to the one Brandie is in, but the woman inside is chained to the shackles on the wall, her feet barely touching the ground. She's naked and there's no IV pole, although judging by the way her head lolls to the side, she's unconscious and drugged.

I whirl around and advance on Luciano, pinning him to the opposite wall with my forearm pressed against his throat. The grin never leaves his face, even as he tries to suck in air. I hear a gun cock and feel the barrel press against the back of my head, but I ignore it.

"I gotta say, I thought you'd appreciate this a little more," Luciano sneers.

"And why would you think that?"

"Because Kitty Kat is no longer your problem."

25

JETT

"What's the end game here?"

Jackson is dangerously close to killing Luciano, consequences be damned. I need to get things back on track. Normally, I'd defer to my boss, but Kevin Vick is frozen stupid.

"What do you think?" Luciano sneers. "Money. Power. Same as—"

"You already have those!" Mr. Vick finally finds his voice. He glances at the man with a gun pointed at Jackson's head. "Put the fucking gun down. We both know you're not gonna shoot him."

The guy looks to his boss, who nods his head as much as he's able with Jackson holding him the way he is. The weapon is lowered slowly, and the goon doesn't look happy about it.

"Jack, let him go." Now that Mr. Vick has recovered his balls, his voice is laced with authority.

"You said she was mine." Jackson doesn't make a move to release Luciano. "I told you, I don't share."

"I told you she was yours until she wasn't," Mr. Vick

snaps. "Do I have to remind you what happens when orders aren't followed?"

Jackson holds Luciano for a brief moment longer before shoving away from him. Luciano maintains his calm, unruffled demeanor, as he steps away from the wall and straightens his suit jacket.

"Now that the unpleasantries are out of the way, shall we discuss business?"

"Why is Kitty Kat here?" Mr. Vick asks.

Luciano shrugs. "Seemed only fair after that set-up at your club."

"If you'll recall, you weren't the one arrested. Why would I set you up only to be taken into custody myself?"

Luciano appears to think about the question.

Wanting to move things along, I say, "With all due respect Mr. Luciano, there was no set-up. We were all arrested and the only reason we're out is because the cops can't do their jobs." I pause, waiting for Mr. Vick to interject with rage at my blatant disregard for my place. "Can we just get down to business? The smell of this place is starting to make me sick."

"Business," Luciano scoffs. "Sure, we can get down to business."

He starts walking back down the hall in the direction we came from but enters a door at about the halfway point. Mr. Vick, Luciano's goon, and I follow him. I glance over my shoulder to see Jackson frozen in front of the door leading to Katelyn.

I can't imagine what this is like for him. I made it a point to learn his history after learning he's FBI. What happened to his family is tragic and no doubt fueling his current actions. I watch as he wraps his fingers around the bars and see his lips move. He lingers for a second, and when he turns to join us, his face is etched with rage.

I have to swallow past the lump in my throat as he stalks

toward me. I've never been so grateful to have someone's anger directed at something other than me because I'm pretty sure Jackson could kill someone right now with his bare hands.

"We need to end this," he whispers fiercely when he reaches my side.

I nod and we enter the room to listen to the 'business' discussion together. Mr. Vick and Luciano are seated across from each other at a metal desk, and they seem to be joking around, not discussing crime world domination. I catch movement out of the corner of my eye and swing my head to see what it is.

Sapphire is standing there in her stripper get-up. *What the fuck is she doing here?* I nudge Jackson with my elbow and tip my head toward her. He quickly looks, and his face turns an alarming shade of red.

"I see my daughter has caught your eye," Luciano says.

Daughter?

Mr. Vick tenses at that bit of information, clearly taken by surprise. I don't know if he noticed Sapphire in the corner when he entered the room but he definitely didn't know she was Luciano's daughter.

"Sapphire coordinates and cares for the girls." Luciano pins Mr. Vick with his stare. "When she's not dancing for you, of course."

"How the he—"

"Shut up!" Luciano barks. "This is the point where I talk and you listen."

Jackson and I step up behind Mr. Vick, offering our muscle like we're supposed to.

"My original offer was forty percent of any and all future profits from The White Lily, as well as access to any stripper I choose." Mr. Vick nods in agreement. "I'm amending my terms."

Luciano stands and joins his daughter, wrapping his arm around her in a way that makes them seem more like lovers than father and daughter.

"I still want forty percent of future profits and access to the strippers. In addition, I want you to obtain a minimum of seventy-five percent of your girls from me, for a fee of course." Luciano smiles at Sapphire. "I'll let you tell them the rest, honey."

"I want to be the opening and closing act. I want to train every girl brought into the club and the girls that you don't purchase from daddy? I have the right to, shall we say, convert them to the escort side of the business and take fifty percent of all money they earn."

"That's ludicrous!" Mr. Vick shoots up from his chair so fast it tips over, the metal clanging on the floor. "You'll have your hands in everything but my drug operation."

"Oh, did I forget that part?" Luciano asks and tilts his head. "You've got a pretty incredible thing going with the drugs, I'll give you that. And lucky for you, I don't want any of the profits from those sales. I'm not a monster, after all. But I do want you to keep me stocked in *supplies* to keep my girls in line."

Jackson and I have everything we need to end this, right here, right now, but it's like a damn train wreck. Neither of us can take our eyes off the spectacle in front of us.

"What's in it for me?" Mr. Vick appears to be weighing his options.

"You don't know?" Sapphire says in a saccharine sweet voice.

Mr. Vick shakes his head.

"Your empire will stand for another day." Luciano smiles. "Don't agree and I will burn it to the ground."

26

KATELYN

"Here kitty kitty."

Sapphire's voice sounds like fingernails on a chalkboard. I try to open my eyes, look toward where it's coming from, but it feels impossible, like a weight has been settled onto my eyelids. The tingling in my hands is painful, and when I make the effort to pull them into my body, they won't move.

"Here kitty kitty."

She's taunting me, toying with me. When I don't respond the way she wants, her laughter disappears and the crack of her palm against my cheek echoes in the space around me. My head whips to the side, and my eyes surge open.

It takes a moment for my blurred vision to clear, and when it does, terror washes over me. I struggle against the chains at my wrists, and my body sways as I do.

"Where the hell am I?" My voice is raspy, my throat bone dry.

"You're home." Sapphire walks toward me, and I turn my face away. She grips my chin, forcing me to look at her, and I know there will be bruises where her fingers squeeze. "You think you're so special, better than everybody else. But I've got news for you," she leans in close and when she speaks again, it's with deadly calm. "Just because you're fucking the help doesn't mean you're safe."

She shoves my head back, and it slams against the wall I'm chained to. Pain explodes in my skull, and my vision blurs again. I blink several times to bring her back into focus. Deep breaths help to control the nausea.

"Are you sure about that?" Jackson will figure out I'm missing. He'll save me.

"I'm pretty sure, considering he's already been here to see you and you're still chained up."

No!

"Why are you doing this?" It doesn't matter why, not really, but I don't know what else to do.

Sapphire stares at me, her eyes void of any emotion, her smile pure evil. How long has she been a part of this? How did I not see this side of her? Sure, she's always been a bitch, but psychotic? Not that I saw.

"Because I can. I own you." She walks toward me, her spiked heels clacking on the floor. "Fun fact: Luciano is my father." She trails a manicured nail down my cheek. I try to pull away but am unsuccessful. "Daddy will do anything to make me happy. And this," she breathlessly whispers as she digs a nail into my flesh. "This makes me practically giddy."

Sapphire's giggle echoes as she exits the room, and the door bangs shut behind her. As soon as she's gone, I crane my neck to take in my surroundings. There's a stainless steel table that is reminiscent of a veterinarian's examination table. A fluorescent light illuminates the room, but it's flickering, which only serves to intensify my headache. There are no windows, and if my failing struggles are any indication, there's no escaping my shackles.

Blood trickles down my arms from where the metal has

dug into my wrists and broken skin. My legs are numb from dangling, and my stomach is well past the stage of being in knots. I try to listen for any sound, but all I hear is deafening silence.

I know Jackson will do whatever it takes to save me but when? How long will I have to be here, like this, before he shows up? I break out in a sweat, and I'm not sure if it's from the fear or whatever Sapphire shot me up with. I let my eyes slide closed. No need to stare at nothing. Besides, I'm tired and my brain isn't firing on all cylinders. Maybe if I rest for a bit, I'll be able to think more clearly.

The door slams against the wall, jolting me. My eyes fly open and land on Sapphire, standing just inside the doorway, a garment bag draped over her arm.

"Time to get ready," she sing-songs as she makes her way toward me.

Sapphire is no longer wearing the stripper garb I'm used to. A blue satin dress hugs her curves, the color complimenting her skin tone. Her feet are encased in strappy stiletto heels, and her legs seem to go on forever beneath the almost hip high slit.

"Get ready for what?" I lock eyes with her and cringe when I see the evil that was there earlier mixed with a hint of... desire?

"Daddy has guests and he wants to show off our new acquisition." Her eyes roam down my body, stopping when they reach the juncture between my thighs. "Personally, I don't think you're ready, but daddy's in charge."

"I'm not going anywhere with you."

Her palm connects with my cheek. "You will do as you're told." She sighs, like she's carrying the weight of the world on her shoulders. "Kitty Kat, don't make this harder than it has to be."

"You think I'm just going to sit back and make this easy for you?"

"I think," she pauses for dramatic effect, "you don't have much of a choice unless you want to spend your time here drugged. This can be a very lucrative opportunity for you, Kitty Kat. You should enjoy it."

"No thanks."

"Have it your way then," she says.

Sapphire walks to the stainless steel table and yanks open a drawer. *How had I missed that?* When she turns around, there's a syringe in her hand. I thrash my head from side to side and yank against the confines of my restraints.

"What are you doing?" I demand.

"Doing this your way." She brings the syringe up to her mouth and pulls the cap off with her teeth before spitting it to the ground. Sapphire jabs the needle into my neck and depresses the plunger. "Don't worry, Kitty Kat. You'll learn… eventually."

Whatever she injected seems to burn a path through my veins. I fight to keep my eyes open, but it's a losing battle.

"How much did you give her?"

The voice sounds vaguely familiar, but I can't quite place it.

"She refused to do what she was told. I had no choice."

That lying voice belongs to Sapphire. She sounds like she's pouting, and it's a stark contrast to the bitch that shot me up with drugs. I slowly slide back into consciousness as I listen to the conversation around me. When I'm able to open my eyes, I see who she's talking to and chastise myself for not recognizing the voice.

"Baby, I'm sorry. You know how your father is. This has to be just right or the deal is off."

Stoner slides his hand up her thigh and squeezes her ass. Sapphire moans before

jumping up and wrapping her legs around his waist. He catches her easily and backs her against the wall. They're oblivious to the fact that they now have an audience. When Sapphire's hands go to Stoner's belt and she starts to undo it, I can't remain silent.

"Do you mind?" I snap.

They both chuckle, but they do break apart. Stoner stalks toward me and pulls me up from the cot I'm lying on. He walks a circle around me, and I swear I can feel every spot his gaze touches like a physical blow.

"Gotta say, Sapphy, you did good." Stoner wraps his meaty fingers around my bicep and drags me across the room to stand in front of a mirror. "Did she do good, Kitty Kat?"

I don't recognize the woman staring back at me. My honey-blonde hair is dyed black and accented by a headband with cat ears. My lips are painted black and there are whiskers drawn on my cheeks, stemming from my pink-tipped nose. My arms are encased in black fur gloves, and the black leather dress has slits on both sides that put Sapphire's dress to shame.

Stoner spins me around so I can look at the view of the back. It's equally horrifying. My back is exposed entirely. A long black fur tail is attached to my ass. I glance down at my feet to see black stiletto heels with ribbons that lace up around my ankles.

I swallow past the lump in my throat. I've dressed in far less fabric than this and then stripped it off for horny men, yet somehow, this is more demeaning.

"Why?" I croak.

"This is how tonight is going to go." Sapphire steps between me and the mirror. The sound of leather snapping reaches my ears, and that's when I notice the flogger she's holding. "Daddy is still trying to close the deal with Mr. Vick. The little fuck is being stubborn and his minions aren't helping the situation. So, you're going to join us all for dinner and you're going to convince your fuck buddy that you're exactly where you want to be."

"He'll never believe that."

"He will if you play your part." Stoner forces me to turn around and face him. "If Jack isn't convinced, there will be consequences." Leather slices into my back, and I cry out in pain. "Not only for you, but for me, as well. And I don't like consequences." Another stinging whip.

"You see, Daddy doesn't like to get his hands dirty, just like Mr. Vick. And if this deal doesn't happen, daddy has made a promise to burn Mr. Vick's operation to the ground."

"So," I challenge, tears streaming down my cheeks.

"So, if Mr. Vick needs to be *shut down*, I'm the one that will have to do it," Stoner answers for her.

"Which opens him up for consequences of his own and we don't want that." Sapphire's tone is reminiscent of a school girl. "*I* don't want that. My man can't go to jail again."

"You're a decent stripper." Stoner grins. "Now we need you to be an excellent actress."

27

JACKSON

"Where the hell is Slade?"

I glance around the ornate dining room. Mr. Vick and Luciano are seated at either end of the table. Other than them, there are place settings for six more individuals. Three on either side of the eight-foot table. Jett and I have yet to sit down. I'd made a scene about not sitting down until everyone had arrived. For security reasons, of course.

"I don't know," I whisper to Jett. "I've pushed this damn button so many times and even if I hadn't, he should have heard enough to come in with the team."

"We've been here for hours. We should just finish this ourselves."

He's right, we should. But we have no weapons, no restraints to make the arrest, nothing. That's why we had the plan we had.

"Let's just see who is joining us for dinner and go from there."

I hate the words coming out of my mouth. I don't want to wait. All I want to do is rush back to the east wing and get

Katelyn the fuck out of here. But I can't. Not yet. We've been thrown one loop after another since we arrived and there's no telling what others we'll be thrown.

Jett and I stand in silence for a few more minutes, taking in everything, listening to the conversation between Mr. Vick and Luciano. Mr. Vick is scared shitless. He knows that Luciano has him over a barrel, and at this point, he's just doing what he has to in order to stay afloat. If it weren't for Jett and I doing what we had to do to stall, he would have already agreed to Luciano's deal and would probably be home in bed.

And we'd be screwed because Slade isn't following through with his part of the plan. I depress the button on my watch... again.

"Ah, there you are."

Luciano rises from his seat and walks across the room, disappearing behind an ornate piece of furniture. Jett and I exchange a quick look but focus our attention on the place where Luciano will appear again.

When Luciano reappears, he's followed by Sapphire, the conniving cunt, and another face I wasn't prepared to see. It's impossible to miss the flogger that Sapphire is carrying. Stoner has his arm wrapped around Sapphire's waist and shakes Luciano's hand with his free one.

"Didn't see that coming," Jett whispers.

"Traitors! I'm surrounded by traitors." Mr. Vick is up out of his chair, and his wine glass shatters as it hits the wall. He whirls on Jett and me. "What about you two? Are you next?"

"No, sir."

Jett and I respond simultaneously.

"Kevin, Kevin, Kevin. Did you really think this was a game you'd win?" Luciano quirks a brow. Mr. Vick bristles at his tone. "Now, sit down and shut up. We need to finish our business."

Luciano returns to his chair and seats himself. Sapphire and Stoner sit on one side of the table, with an empty chair between them. Mr. Vick sits back down, and Jett and I take our seats across from the two who's betrayal shouldn't surprise me. Nothing should surprise me anymore.

Sapphire's eyes lock with mine, and they seem to glitter with excitement.

"Here kitty kitty," she calls over her shoulder, her gaze never wavering.

I let my gaze travel beyond Sapphire, to the door where she and Stoner entered and rage washes over me until I'm seeing red. Katelyn, defeated and dehumanized, walks toward the table. Tears stain her cheeks, and she's visibly shaking. Her eyes are bloodshot and her gait unstable.

"Jesus Christ," Jett murmurs under his breath.

"Kitty Kat," Luciano prompts and she turns her head to look at him. "Please, have a seat." He gestures with his arm to indicate the empty chair between Stoner and Sapphire.

Katelyn does as she's told, and just when I think she's not going to make eye contact, she raises her head and focuses on me. My heart shatters as my dead wife's image seems to transpose over Katelyns. I failed Melinda and Benny years ago, and here I am again, failing to protect the woman I love.

Luciano snaps his fingers and trays of food are immediately brought to the table. Brandie is among the four women serving us. She's dressed, which is a vast improvement on the other times I've seen her. She's also smiling, but it doesn't reach her eyes. She's not fooling anyone.

"This looks delicious," Luciano praises his 'staff', who are now lined up along the wall waiting to be summoned.

Everyone begins eating. Everyone but Katelyn and me. My blood is boiling, and the longer I look at her, the harder it becomes to keep myself in check.

"You have a funny way of trying to seal a deal," Mr. Vick scoffs.

I lose the battle and my shit in the span of a few seconds.

I lunge up from my chair and swipe my arm across the table, sending everything in front of me flying to the floor. I allow myself to look at Jett and at that moment, I know, he's got my back.

"FBI!"

"DEA!"

The doors behind us crash against the wall, and I whirl around. Slade and his team, along with who I assume are Jett's guys, are surrounding the table, guns drawn.

It's about damn time.

"You're under arrest for..."

Jett's words fade away as I stare at Katelyn, who has yet to react to the chaos. Out of the corner of my eye, I catch a glimpse of Slade slapping cuffs on Kevin Vick. A week ago—hell, an hour ago—I would have fought him for that privilege, but right now, I care about nothing other than the woman across from me.

"You will regret this," Vick sneers as Slade hauls him past me and toward the exit.

"Hold up," I call out to Slade, stopping him in his tracks.

I stand toe to toe with the man I've spent the last year trying to bring down. He stares at me with disgust, like I'm the one who's made this world a hellish place.

"You really have no idea who I am?" I tilt my head, genuinely interested in his answer. I don't know why my tone sounds as if I'm surprised. I shouldn't be. I was overseas when my family was murdered, and he wasn't the one to actually pull the trigger.

"Should I?" he challenges.

"Probably not." I shrug like it's no big deal while inside,

I'm coiled tighter than a snake about to strike. "I'm going to enlighten you though."

"What? Did someone you love overdose or something?"

He's taunting me with a smug grin. I pull my arm back and clench my fist. When it connects with his jaw, he howls in pain as blood dribbles down his chin. He struggles against his cuffs, trying to get to me, but Slade holds him firm.

"You saw that! He hit me. I wanna file charges." Vick's eyes are wild, crazed.

Slade looks at me and winks. "I didn't see anything." He surveys the room and sees that Katelyn is the only one remaining, other than the three of us. "I think I'm just going to go check on my men. Jackson, you got this?"

It takes a second for his words to register and when they do, I feel the corners of my mouth tug up. "Yeah. Yeah, I got this."

I crack my knuckles and wait for Slade to walk out of sight. He has to know that this isn't exactly going to end the way the Bureau wants. I make a mental note to buy the man a drink later. Hell, I'll buy his drinks for the next ten years if that's what it takes to make us even.

"I've dreamt about this moment for a long time." I advance on Vick, and he takes a step back. I let him, wanting him to think he can get away from me. "You see, you know me as Jack Duffy but my name is Jackson Stark." When there's no indication that the name sounds familiar, I continue. "I had a wife, Melinda, and a son, Benny."

I grab Vick by the arm and yank him back to the table, shoving him into a chair. He lets out a 'humph' when his ass hits the wood. I glance at Katelyn, and she's still just sitting there, although she looks more alert and there's a glint in her eye. It's not a lot but it's enough to let me know that she's going to be okay.

"Darlin', this is about to get ugly." I gauge her reaction. "You okay with that?"

Her gaze darts back and forth between me and Vick. Her lips quirk up and she nods.

I grab Vick by his hair and yank his head back. "Buckle up, buttercup. Your world is about to crumble." I slam his face into the table.

Katelyn stands up and places her palms on the table, leaning forward. "You are a sick bastard, and while I want nothing more than to watch you pay, I think I'm gonna leave this to Jackson."

Vick says nothing and since I'm behind him, I can't see his reaction. Katelyn walks around the table and steps up to me, wrapping her arms around my waist. I make no move to return the gesture. I'm too wound up and afraid I'd hurt her.

"I'll be outside." Katelyn stands on her tip-toes and places a quick kiss on my cheek. "Give him hell."

I listen to her footsteps as she retreats and leaves me alone with my enemy. For a brief moment, I consider following her, letting the justice system sort out Vick's fate. I quickly dismiss that thought. I've waited too long for this, and I'm not giving it up for anything. Not even for Katelyn.

"I will have your badge," Vick shouts. "Think about this. I will end you and your career. I will bury you!"

I chuckle at his optimism. He still thinks he's getting out of here alive. I may not have my weapon, but I've got my hands and steel-toed boots. He's going to wish I had my gun.

Despite having rehearsed what I would say to him when the opportunity presented itself, I feel unprepared. Pissed as hell, but unprepared, so what comes out is random, convoluted.

"I've tried to figure out who was there that night. Which of your guys pulled the trigger." I turn him to face me, chair and all. "I was in the Army. Did you know that? The night they came to my house, I was thousands of miles away, unable to protect them."

Vick's tough demeanor is starting to fall. Not so much that I think he's afraid of me but enough that I know he's starting to grasp that I'm not just any undercover agent.

"We fought before I left. She was going to leave me, take my son. I knew there was a greater than average chance they wouldn't be there when I got home. But they would have been alive." I haul him up and land a punch to his gut. "A quick fix, that's why they died." Another punch to the gut. "You'll kill an infant, a new mother, but you leave the old lady." Another punch and then I drag him to the wall, slamming him against it.

Vick turns his head and spits blood before facing me again. "I just hope they had fun with her first."

I'd wanted to drag this out, make him suffer, but those words are all it takes to bring my plan to a screeching halt. Or carry them out at warp speed, depending on how you look at it.

"Motherfucker!"

I take out years of pent up rage on his face, yelling the entire time. I don't recognize myself, this man who is killing like it's the only way to survive. Vick attempts to fend off my assault, but I'm bigger, stronger. Hell, that's why he hired me.

He slumps to the floor and my punches cease, but I continue to pummel him with my feet. Kicking him in the ribs, the face, everywhere. He's covered in blood, and it's spattering on the wall and floor.

"They were my world," I shout as I keep at it. "You took them from me!"

After what feels like hours, I fall to my knees. Vick isn't breathing and I lean forward to check his pulse. There isn't one. I did what I set out to do. I took his life, just like he took mine.

I sit back on my haunches and let my head fall back. My eyes are closed, but I can see. I see my wife, sitting in a rocking chair, nursing our son.

"I did it, Mel," I whisper.

28

KATELYN

"You can't go back in there."

"Try and stop me."

I walk away from Slade and Jett. They managed to get everyone into the awaiting vehicles and sent on their way to the jail, but we stayed behind to wait on Jackson. There was no need to worry about transporting Mr. Vick. We all knew he wouldn't be going anywhere but the morgue.

"Katelyn," Slade calls from behind me. I halt and glance over my shoulder. Apparently he finally gets that he can't stop me and says, "We'll be out here, waiting."

I nod and continue walking. I still feel a little out of it from whatever Stoner and Sapphire plunged into my veins, but I focus on getting to my destination. My back is on fire from the flogger. I refused treatment, promising Jett and Slade that I would go to the hospital once I had Jackson.

When I step into the dining room where we left him, Jackson is on his knees, his face pointed to the ceiling.

"I did it, Mel." His voice cracks as he whispers.

"Jackson?" I step up behind him and put my hand on his

shoulder. He flinches at the contact, and his eyes fly open and land on me. "It's over." I nod toward the limp, bloody body in front of him.

"I couldn't save them." His eyes glisten and tears slide down his cheeks. "They're dead because I left them alone."

I drop to the floor behind him and wrap my arms around his chest, pulling him toward me. I rest my cheek between his shoulder blades and feel the thump, thump, thump of his rapid heartbeat. I focus on that sound and ignore the intense sting of the injuries on my back.

"It's not your fault," I murmur.

Jackson and I sit there, silent other than the sound of his crying. I do the only thing I can: whisper reassurances and hold him through it. Eventually he calms. He links his fingers with mine and squeezes.

"I'm so sorry."

"For what?"

He has nothing to be sorry for. I pull my arms away and urge him to turn around and face me. The utter devastation in his eyes is almost my undoing.

"I didn't protect you." He refuses to look at me. "I should have been at the club with you. You never would have been…"

His words trail off, and his eyes slide closed. I reach out and place my palm on his cheek. He leans into my touch and simultaneously covers my hand with his, holding me there.

"Jackson, look at me." He slowly opens his eyes. "I'll be fine. I *am* fine." I smile at him. "Why don't we head on out?"

Jackson glances over his shoulder at Vick, as if he needs to see him one more time to satisfy himself that he's actually dead. His body relaxes and when he turns back around, his eyes are a little clearer. He stands, pulling me to my feet with him. I tilt my head back so I can see his face.

"It's really over," he murmurs. When I nod, he says, "And

you're okay?" I don't realize it until his eyes narrow, but I hesitate. "Katelyn?"

"It's nothing." I try to reassure him, but he's having none of it.

"Clearly it's not nothing." He pulls me toward him and slides his hands from mine, up my arms, over my shoulders and down my back. I hiss at the contact. He freezes and his face turns to stone. "What the…"

He urges me to turn around, but I resist. When I don't budge, he steps around me. I drop my head, tucking my chin into my chest. So much for getting him out of here first.

"Who the fuck did this?" he demands.

"Jackson, I'm fi—"

"Katelyn," he snaps. "I swear to God if you say you're fine, I'm gonna—"

"What?" I whirl around. "You're gonna what, Jackson? Beat me? Kill someone?" His eyes widen at the vehemence in my tone. "There's been enough of that for one day, don't ya think?"

He stares at me for a long moment before his lips curve into a smile. I narrow my eyes when he chuckles. There's nothing funny about this.

"What the hell is so funny?"

He shakes his head and his expression sobers. "Nothing. It's just…"

"It's just what?"

"You're incredible." He steps closer and puts his hand on the back of my head, pulling me toward him. When his lips touch my forehead, my shoulders slump, all of my fight gone.

Now that the adrenaline has worn off and I know Jackson is okay, I've got nothing left. I'm tired, dizzy, nauseous and in so much pain.

"I should have listened to them."

"To who, darlin'?"

"They told me to go to the hospital." My words are starting to slur, and the room is spinning. "Slade and Jett. They tried to tell me…"

Jackson bends and links his fingers at my ass, lifting me up. I wrap my legs around his waist and my arms around his neck. Relief washes over me at the fact that he figured out a way to carry me without touching my back. I rest my head on his shoulder.

"So tired," I mumble into his neck.

"I've got you."

Jackson carries me out of the room. I try to hold on to consciousness, try to stay awake until we make it outside.

"I've got you, Katelyn."

I hear his words as he says them over and over. I can't speak, don't want to. I can think though, even if my thoughts are a little muddled.

And all I keep thinking is *yeah, you sure as hell do.*

∼

"I love her, man. It's as simple as that."

Jackson's voice is muffled, like I'm underwater and he's just above me. I'm on my stomach, and I register a beeping sound.

"I get it. Really, I do. But what about your career?" Slade sounds frustrated. I haven't known him long, but I imagine he's shoving a frustrated hand through his hair.

"I don't give a fuck about my career." Jackson's getting angry. "I made that mistake once. I won't do it again."

Wait. What?

"You can have both, ya know?"

"Yeah? And how well did that work out for you?"

I manage to open my eyes and turn my head, my gaze

landing on the two of them, standing there, in each other's faces.

"Don't bring them into this."

"Guys," I croak. They don't hear me.

"You're making no fucking sense. One minute you're telling me that I need to think about my career and the next you're telling me I can have her *and* my career. Which is it?"

"Both." Slade huffs out a breath. "You can have a life and a career. I'm just not so sure you can have *her* and *this* career. She's part of the investigation, man."

Jackson's fists clench at his sides, and I know he's close to knocking Slade out.

"Guys!" I shout, as loud as is possible.

Their heads whip toward me. Jackson rushes to my side and brushes a hand over my hair. I try to roll to my side so I can see them more easily, but it's difficult. Jackson helps until I'm situated in a somewhat comfortable position.

"Hey, darlin'." Jackson sits in the chair next to the hospital bed. "How ya feeling?"

"Like I've been drugged and whipped."

"I'll go see if they can give you anything more for the pain." Slade turns on his heel and walks out of the room.

I watch him go as I recount everything I overheard. When I return my gaze to Jackson, I notice the bags under his eyes, the pallor of his skin.

"Are you okay?"

"Of course," he assures me.

"You don't look okay."

"It's just been a long couple of days." He takes a deep breath, holds it for a second before blowing it out. "I was worried about you."

"A couple of days? I've been here that long?" I don't remember anything after being carried away from Vick's body.

"You've been in and out of it. Mostly out."

"And you've been here—"

"The whole time." He quirks his lips. "I couldn't leave."

"Because you love me?" I hold my breath after the words are out.

"You heard that?" I nod. "Is that a problem?"

I shake my head. "But what about your career?" I don't want to be the reason that he gives up a piece of himself.

"Do you love me?"

"I…" It's on the tip of my tongue to lie. To tell him that I don't so he doesn't throw away his life. But I can't lie, not about this. "Yeah. Yeah, I love you."

"Then we'll sort the rest out."

Slade walks in with a doctor. While I'm being checked over, Jackson backs away and he and Slade retreat to the corner. I'm given more pain meds, and the doctor leaves, saying he'll be back later to check on me.

Jackson returns to my side and just before the meds suck me under, I hear him whisper 'I love you' one last time.

29

JACKSON

"I don't want to go."

Katelyn's arm is thrown across my stomach and her head is resting in the crook of my neck. Waking up with her by my side is a pleasure that took some getting used to. Not that I don't want her here, but there's a part of me that still questions whether or not I deserve her.

"I know you don't." I kiss the top of her head, letting my lips linger for a moment. "Quite frankly, neither do I. I'd much rather stay in bed with you."

I pull her on top of me, and she straddles my hips. When she leans to kiss me, her golden hair hangs down, framing my face and seems to shut out our surroundings. When she was released from the hospital, she begged me to take her to a salon to have her hair dyed back to her natural color. I run my fingers through her locks and apply pressure at the back of her head, holding her to me.

"Let's just stay here," she purrs when she breaks the kiss.

She sits up straight and grabs the hem of her tank top, pulling it up and over her head. Her pebbled nipples are practically pointing at me, and I reach out to pinch them between my thumbs and forefingers. She throws her head back at the contact, and when I sit up and draw one into my mouth, she moans.

I release her nipples and lean close to her ear. I suck the lobe and nibble, my cock straining as the sounds coming from her grow louder.

"I wanna bury myself in you," I growl.

She wraps her fist around my dick and gives it a tug. I've never been more grateful that I sleep naked than I am at this moment. She works me until pre-cum beads at my tip. With her free hand, she reaches down to slide her red lace panties out of the way and guides me to her opening.

I'm watching her face as her pussy swallows me up. Hooded eyes stare back at me. Katelyn rocks her hips, gliding over me in deliriously slow motion. I press my thumb into her clit and her walls immediately clench. I want to flip her over, fuck her hard into the mattress, but her back is still healing so I let her do her thing, savoring the sweet, slow burn.

"Ah, Katelyn, come for me." My voice is gritty, need driving my words.

She increases her pace, her tits bouncing with every movement. She reaches behind her to play with my balls. Her tongue darts out for a second before she draws her bottom lip between her teeth. Katelyn pulls my hand from her hip and wraps her mouth around my finger, sucking, licking, moaning around it. The vibrations rush through my hand, travel down my arm, all the way to my dick.

I know I'm close to losing it, but I can't go without her. I use both of my hands and massage her breasts, tweak her nipples. Katelyn reaches between us and rubs her bundle of nerves. Watching her pleasure herself, while I'm balls deep, is erotic, torturous, not likely to slow down the oncoming freight train of my release.

"I, I'm… oh sweet Jesus," she pants. "Gonna come."

Her fingers are flying, assaulting her clit while her hips are racing. I thrust to meet her every move, both of us chasing a frenzied release. Her pussy spasms around me, and my body tenses. Colors dance in front of my face as my orgasm soars. Katelyn's moans are fucking beautiful, but they're nothing compared to the way her face completely opens up and every feeling is there for me to see.

She collapses on top of me when the quivering slows. I roll us both so we're on our sides, facing each other. I push a strand of hair behind her ear so I can see her satisfied, sleepy smile. Her eyes are closed, and I hate to ruin the moment but know that we can't stop the inevitable.

"Darlin', we should probably get ready."

"Mmm."

I sit up and use the sheet to wipe myself clean before turning my attention to her. She squirms while I dry her off, but her eyes never open. I toss the sheet to the floor so I don't forget to throw it in the washer and make my way to the shower in the adjoining bathroom. I'll let her rest for a few minutes.

I adjust the water temperature before stepping in and letting it rain over me. My head is tipped back, and my eyes are closed when I hear the footsteps. The glass door opens and small arms wrap around my waist. Katelyn presses her cheek into my chest and I wrap my arms around her waist. We stand like that for several minutes, and it takes everything in me to step away.

We take turns under the spray, and when we're done, we dry off and finish getting ready. She's putting on her makeup, and I can't help but to watch her reflection in the mirror.

The first time I saw her get ready in the morning had been a revelation.

Kitty Kat had been a sex symbol, dark hair, dark make-up. She'd been created to seduce. The woman looking at me in the mirror is her exact opposite. Katelyn is gorgeous and doesn't need a drop of make-up but chooses to wear it to 'enhance' her already naturally perfect features.

Our eyes connect in the reflective glass and she smiles. I'll never tire of seeing that, the evidence of pure happiness, especially since I know I put it there. She tells me so all the time.

My cell phone rings from the other room, breaking the spell. When I make no move to go answer it, she nudges me with her elbow. I shake my head and walk into the bedroom, swiping my phone off the nightstand.

"Hello," I answer.

"We'll be there in five." Slade's tone is clipped.

"Got it. We're ready."

I end the call and glance up as Katelyn steps into the room. "They're almost here."

Her eyes light up with excitement, as they always do when she knows she's going to see Brandie. Our boss doesn't like the fact that Katelyn and I are together, but he recognizes that I can keep her safe, which is imperative until the trial. He assigned Slade to watch over Brandie so she'd be with him today.

By the time Slade lays on the horn to signal their arrival, Katelyn and I are standing by the door, ready to go. Brandie is in the backseat so I climb in up front with Slade. His jaw is hard, and his shoulders are stiff with tension.

"Hey guys," Katelyn chirps when she gets in next to Brandie.

I glance over my shoulder and catch Brandie's forced

smile. She's sitting as close to the door as she can possibly get, her hands folded in her lap. It's been a little over two weeks since we sprung her from hell, and while she's made some improvements, she's still a shell of the woman Katelyn talks about.

I settle into my seat and stare out the window as Slade drives us to the courthouse. Katelyn's voice floats through the SUV as she chats with, or more accurately, *at* Brandie. I watch Slade out of the corner of my eye, see his hands flex on the steering wheel, his head go from side to side as he tries to ease the tension in his neck. Satisfied that Katelyn's talking will drown my words out, I break the silence in the front.

"How are things going?" I ask Slade. He shrugs. "Still no progress?"

"She's infuriating." Anger simmers just below the surface of his words. "I try to make conversation and get nothing. I can't do this. Not for as long as it could take for the trial to actually start. She hates me."

"Man, she's traumatized. I wouldn't take it personally." I have no idea what to say to him. He's stuck with an almost catatonic victim, and I feel a little guilty because protecting Katelyn is hardly difficult.

"Kinda hard to not take it personally when the only time she speaks is to scream at me." He takes a deep breath and his cheeks puff out when he blows it out. "And, get this, she likes to throw shit. At my fucking head."

I chuckle at the indignation in his tone. In the time I've known Slade, he's had zero trouble with women, so it's no surprise that Brandie is driving him insane.

"What did she throw at you?" His knuckles whiten as his grip tightens with my question. "Did you deserve it?" Okay, now I'm just having fun.

"Yes, he deserved it!" Brandie shouts from the back. So

much for her not hearing or talking. "He left his *work* on the table where I'd see it. Like I want to see pictures to remind me of everything. And it was a plate." When I look at her with a quirked brow, she clarifies. "What I threw at his head. It was a goddamn plate."

Katelyn and I lock eyes and then burst into laughter. Brandie's gaze darts between the two of us and she huffs out a breath.

"What? It didn't hit him."

That only makes us laugh harder. Slade clearly doesn't see the hilarity of the situation. He scowls at me, and I have to force myself to sober. The rest of the drive is silent, not even Katelyn chatters to ease the tension.

Ten minutes later, Slade pulls into the courthouse parking lot, expertly winding his way toward the back entrance. The media is camped out front and there's no reason to expose Katelyn and Brandie to that.

Katelyn has tried to shield her family, other than her brother, from everything that's happened and they didn't need to see her face plastered on their television. The hearings were closed, so no cameras or random Joe Schmo's chasing the gory details would be present.

Slade and Brandie walk in front of us, and it's hard to miss the fact that his hand is at the small of her back. For all his bluster, he isn't shirking his responsibility and it seems he might actually be enjoying it. Brandie is leaning slightly toward him, not cringing or screaming like the timid victim turned spitfire I observed on the way here.

"She likes him," Katelyn says matter-of-factly.

"What?" My head whips to the side to stare at her, incredulous at her words.

"Brandie likes Slade." Exasperation is heavy in her tone.

"Darlin', I think you've got your emotions confused. She hates him."

"No, she's afraid of him. Well, maybe not *him*, specifically." She shrugs. "But she doesn't hate him. There's a difference between fear and hate."

"Yeah, I get that but—"

"Just wait. You'll see."

Katelyn interlocks her fingers with mine and we enter the building and ascend up the steps toward the room we were told to go to. Slade and Brandie sit as far apart as the small table will allow, forcing Katelyn and me to take seats opposite one another.

It feels like a western showdown, and I breathe a sigh of relief when the prosecutor walks in. He reviews the facts of the case against Luciano, Sapphire and Stoner with us and way before I'm ready, Katelyn is led away to give her testimony.

Slade tries to make small talk, Brandie sits in silence, and I worry. I hate that I can't be in the courtroom with Katelyn. I despise that she has to face her demons alone. Why the three of them are being tried together is beyond me, but they've got the best team of attorneys money can buy and I guess they pulled some strings.

When Katelyn returns to the room, her eyes are red and I can tell she's been crying. I immediately rise and wrap her in my arms. She cries for a moment before pulling herself together and stepping back to look up at me.

"That was brutal," she murmurs.

"I know."

"No, you don't." She shakes her head and throws a worried look at Brandie. "They twisted every word I said. I'm scared, Jackson. I thought this was going to be a no-brainer, but now I'm not so sure. What if they get off?"

"That's not going to happen." I ease her into the chair next to her friend and glance at Slade. "We won't let it."

I don't know if that's true, if Slade, Jett and I have enough in our files to make the charges stick, but I do know one thing.

If they're released, I will hunt them down and do to them what I did to Vick.

30

KATELYN

Four months later...

"We the jury, find the defendant, Saul Luciano, guilty of all charges."

I slump against Jackson with relief. It's been a long time coming, although it could have been longer. We'd all been grateful when the trial was scheduled quickly, and now it seems to have paid off. We're finally free of Luciano.

With him behind bars and Vick dead, Slade can bring Brandie out of hiding—wherever that might be—and Jackson and I can focus on our relationship. Things have been incredible with him, but there's always been this cloud hanging over our heads. It'll be interesting to see what life is like when it's… normal.

"We the jury, find the defendant, Sapphire Luciano, not guilty of all charges."

Jackson stiffens and his arms tighten around me, making

it difficult to breathe. How is this possible? She kidnapped me, drugged me, beat me, and she gets to go home?

"We the jury, find the defendant, Gary Jones, aka Stoner, not guilty of all charges."

Chaos erupts around me as one side of the courtroom cheers and the other yells about the injustice of it all. Voices are muffled, and my lungs hurt as I try to suck in air. At some point, Jackson guides me out of the room and down the hall to an empty, quiet corner.

"Darlin', breathe," he croons.

He rubs circles over my back. My injuries have long since healed, and I'm left with nothing but ugly scars and torturous nightmares to remind me of the worst few hours of my life. I force myself to focus on his hand, the rhythmic movement calming me.

"How am I going to tell her? What do I say to her to make this right?"

I know the verdict means that I'm not safe, but I have Jackson and I always will. Brandie has been with Slade throughout this whole ordeal, but his protection only lasted until the end of the trial, which is today, now. They chose not to come today because Brandie suffered enough during all of the trial testimony.

"You tell her the truth." Jackson bends down to look me in the eye. "You remind her that she has you and by extension, me, to lean on. It's going to be okay."

"Nothing about this okay. Nothing has been okay since the first time I stepped on stage at The White Lily."

Hurt flashes in Jackson's eyes, but I don't have it in me to correct myself, to reassure him that I'm not referring to him. I avert my gaze and he cups my chin, urging me to stop hiding. Before I can, a commotion breaks out down the hall.

We both turn toward it, and I begin to tremble when I see Sapphire and Stoner walking through the same courtroom door that we had. They aren't wearing handcuffs, and aren't surrounded by cops. They're free.

They turn in the opposite direction and head for the elevator, but when they get there, Sapphire glances over her shoulder. Her eyes focus on me and a wicked smile stretches across her face. A shiver races down my spine at the sight.

Jackson and I wait until they disappear before we make any move to leave. We take the back stairs so we can exit the building via a staff entrance. Much like the preliminary hearing, it has been a media circus and there's been security to ensure they don't enter the courthouse, but that hasn't stopped the vulchers from staking out the main entrance.

Jackson holds the door open for me and when the sun hits my face, it feels like a betrayal. This is not a good day, but apparently God's still smiling. Good for him.

I'm ushered to Jackson's car and even though I'm safe behind tinted windows, I don't relax until he's expertly weaved through the downtown traffic of Indianapolis, away from the madness. He makes a few phone calls. I don't eavesdrop, but I can tell based on his side of the conversation that he speaks to his boss and then to Slade.

I realize we aren't going back to his place when he takes the ramp onto I-465. I have no clue where he's headed, but I'm too numb to care. I lean my head against the window and my eyes drift closed.

Maybe if I sleep, my emotions will too.

∼

"Darlin', we're here."

Jackson gently shakes me, thinking I'm sleeping. I had been, but somehow my body knew when the vehicle slowed and I've been awake for a while. I sit up straight and stretch my arms above my head, flattening my palms on the roof of the car as I do.

I glance out the window, trying to ascertain where we are, but nothing is familiar. We're parked in front of a log cabin, which is situated among the trees. There's a motorcycle parked in front of the house, as well as a Jeep, and a swingset in the side yard. The place looks idyllic.

"Where are we?" I turn toward Jackson.

"A friend's place."

He opens his door and rounds the hood of the car to open mine. I grasp his hand when he holds it out for me and let him help me. Jackson leads me to the porch but before we even make it to the door, it's thrown open and a very large, very imposing man steps out. He's hot, in a rough and gritty sort of way, but he doesn't come close to what I see when I look at Jackson.

"You made it," the man says and I recognize his voice but can't quite place it.

"We did."

Jackson and the man shake hands. It seems awkward, yet both men appear to relax after.

"You must be Katelyn."

I nod and dart a confused look at Jackson. He doesn't seem to understand my confusion, and I can tell the moment he figures it out because he chuckles.

"Right, you haven't officially met. Katelyn," Jackson slings an arm around my shoulders. "This is Micah Mallory, president of the Broken Rebel Brotherhood."

It takes me a second for the name to register, and when it does, I launch myself at Micah, throwing my arms around his neck. He catches me easily and hugs me tight. I hold on to him, so much gratitude flowing through me. Jackson clears his throat behind me, and Micah laughs before putting me back on my feet.

"I think we're making him jealous, honey." Laughter dances in Micah's eyes. "And I know my wife would be if she saw that."

"I'm sorry. It's just…" Tears well in my eyes, but for the first time in a long time, they aren't from sadness or fear. "Thank you. You saved my brother, kept my family safe. Thank you."

"It's nothin'." Micah shifts on his feet, appearing uncomfortable. "Why don't you both come inside?"

We follow him in and are led through to the kitchen. He grabs three beers from the refrigerator and motions for us to have a seat at the table. We sit in silence, each drinking, a few sips at a time. Well, I had a few sips. They seemed to both empty their bottles pretty quickly.

"Oh, for fucks sake." Micah slams his bottle on the table top, leans back and folds his arms across his chest. "Are you going to give me an explanation for why you left like you did or not? I've let it go for the sake of all the shit you've had going on, but that's over and I want answers."

Jackson glances at me and then returns his attention to Micah. He takes a deep breath and tips his head back to stare at the ceiling.

"I'm not a patient man, Jackson, so spit it out. Or get out." Micah shrugs. "Your choice."

"You know about my past, what happened to my family," Jackson says after a moment.

"Of course. You lost your shit on my brother, and he forced you to spill your guts. What's

that got to do with why you left?"

"You know about Kevin Vick."

"Jesus Christ, just spit it out," Micah snaps, clearly aggravated at Jackson's cryptic sentences.

"Vick is, *was* responsible for Mel and Benny's murder." Jackson's face is a blank mask, as it always is when he talks about them. "You knew I was leaving for the FBI. I never kept that from you. I hadn't planned on leaving as soon as I did, or without so much as a 'goodbye' but the FBI had an undercover operation they wanted me on. I was going to be the new guy, someone no one had dealt with before. When they asked me to come early and I heard the name of the guy they were trying to take down…"

"You couldn't pass up the opportunity to get revenge," Micah finishes for him.

"Yeah." Jackson hangs his head. When he raises it and speaks, there is a desperate quality to his voice. "Man, I had no choice and even if—"

Micah holds up his hand to silence Jackson. "Did you get revenge?"

Jackson's stare hardenes, but he smiles. "Vick's dead."

Micah gives a tight nod and stands. "Want another beer?"

Jackson narrows his eyes, as if he doesn't believe that's the end of the discussion. "Nah, I'm good."

"Okay." Micah shuts the refrigerator door, not getting anything for himself either. "Why don't we head on over to the main house? That's where the party is."

"Party?" I look between Micah and Jackson. "What party? I'm not dressed for a party." I glance down at my outfit: black slacks, button down blouse. Great for court, not so much for a party.

"You look great." Jackson leans in and kisses my cheek. "But if you want to change, I brought you clothes. They're in the car."

"You did?"

He nods. "Be right back."

Jackson stands and leaves me alone with Micah. Micah seems to dissect me with his stare, and I shift in my chair, feeling exposed.

"So, um… just like that, the past is forgiven?" I don't know how close these two men were prior to Jackson going undercover, but it seems to me it was pretty close and Micah had been really hurt by the perceived betrayal.

"Yep. Just like that." Micah flips his chair around and straddles it. He continues to stare, as if trying to determine if I'm friend or foe. "How much has Jackson told you about the BRB?"

"BRB?" I raise my brows in question.

"Broken Rebel Brotherhood," he clarifies.

"Oh, right. Well, nothing really. I mean, I know you all helped a few months ago and were keeping an eye on my family, but I don't know much beyond that."

"Huh." He looks a little disappointed but seems to rally. "See this?" He points to a patch on his leather vest. "This is who we are. A group of veterans who created a family. We help when and where the law can't." At my confused expression, he continues. "There are a lot of people in this country who are made victims. We help them become survivors. We dole out justice when necessary but for the most part, we protect, we serve, we *help* when there are no other options."

"Wow."

"Jackson was the sheriff here before he went all fed on us. We worked together a lot. He's a good man. But he had a lot of shit going on that he kept to himself. Demons to face." Micah takes a deep breath and shakes his head. "If leaving allowed him to put those demons to rest, then I'm glad he left. I just wish he'd trusted us enough to clue us in."

"I did trust you." Jackson's voice startles me but not Micah. He must have seen him walk in. "But it wasn't your fight. Not that time." Jackson hands me a bag. "Why don't you go change?"

"Bathroom's down the hall, first door on the left." Micah points beyond me indicating the way.

"Thanks."

I grab the bag Jackson packed and head to the bathroom. The hallway is lined with photos of Micah and who I assume are his wife and kids. My heart bleeds as I think of the family Jackson lost, the wife he was supposed to grow old with, the son he should've seen walk across the stage to get his diploma.

As I'm changing into the jeans and long sleeved tee Jackson brought, I wonder if his revenge gave him the closure he needs to move on. Sure, we're happy together and we've had some good times, even though they were colored by the nightmare of our situation.

But do we have what it takes? Can we have a hallway lined with family photos? I don't expect him to forget his past, but can he make a future? With me?

31

JACKSON

"She seems to be doing fine."

I'm watching Katelyn, who's across the room talking with Sadie, Brie and Scarlett. It's good to see her with women who won't hurt her. Brandie is with them, but she's holding back, keeping her distance, emotionally if not physically.

"Yeah, she is." I turn toward the guys and focus on Micah's statement. "She still has nightmares, and you should have seen her when the verdict was read, but she's strong. A fighter."

"Maybe some of that will rub off on Brandie." Slade's eyes are laser focused on Brandie. I can't tell if it's because he still feels responsible for her, as a protector, or if there's more to it. "I think she's out of strength. There's not a drop of fight left in her, unless it's directed at me for some crazy perceived infraction."

I chuckle, remembering her outburst on the way to the preliminary hearing. That girl has a lot more fight in her than Slade realizes.

"I can have Sadie talk to her, if you want," Micah offers.

Sadie is great with victims, and she's made it her mission to be a support for the women the BRB helps. Ever since she arrived, their mission deepened, and became more than what they could have done on their own.

"That'd be great." Slade takes a long pull from his beer. He's brooding and it's hilarious.

"Getting her away from here will go a long way in helping with her state of mind." Griffin slaps Slade on the back. "Just be sure to use the documentation I gave you and destroy anything she has that can link back to her."

"What documentation?" I glare at Slade. "What's he talking about?"

"I'm taking her somewhere." Slade's glare challenges me to argue with him. He's in luck because I have no idea what to even argue about.

"Where? Why?" I shake my head to clear the questions.

"Dude, she's afraid of her own shadow," Slade bellows. Heads turn our way and I can't miss the shocked stare of the woman in question. "She's a pain in my ass, no doubt about it, but you haven't had to watch her every single day since we rescued her. You haven't had to watch her fight me like hell one minute and become a timid mouse the next."

"So, set her up with a shrink, tell her to talk to her best friend. Don't run with her. She's not your responsibility."

I don't know why I'm arguing with him. He's clearly made up his mind. I should be offering support, not alternatives.

"I've got some vacation time saved up. I was waiting to hear the verdict before putting in the request, but as soon as Katelyn gave her the news, I knew what I had to do. We're leaving."

"Where will you go?"

"Don't know." He shrugs. "No where close, that's for sure."

"Katelyn's not going to like this," I mumble. My woman is

going to hate this. She just got her friend back and she's losing her all over again.

"Katelyn has you. She'll be fine. And it's not like we're never going to come back."

"So this is temporary?"

"That's the plan, but as long as Sapphire and Stoner are on the loose, I'll keep her gone."

"I don't get it. You gave me hell about Katelyn, but at least I love her. Why are you doing this?"

"Because." Slade pins me with a hard stare. "It's the right thing to do."

∼

"I hate to say it, but I told ya so."

I down the shot of Jack Daniels in front of me, enjoying the burn as it slides down my throat. When I return my gaze to Katelyn, she's fighting a laugh and it's one of the sexiest things I've ever seen.

"You did." I tuck a strand of hair behind her ear and lean in to whisper, "I wanna punish that smart mouth of yours."

Katelyn shivers at my words, and the whimper that escapes makes it almost impossible to remember we're still at the party and surrounded by people. She sets her beer on the bar and turns to wrap her arms around me.

"As fun as that sounds, I'm not quite ready to leave."

"I know." I grip her arms and urge her back a step. "We can't stay here forever, though."

Katelyn glances around the room, taking in the men and women I call friends. A smile tugs at her lips as she returns her attention to me.

"I feel safe here."

"Everyone feels safe here," I joke, although it's true. "It's part of what makes them so good at what they do." I let out a chuckle. "Well, that and their combined military experience."

"What do we do now?" Her tone turns pensive and her wrinkled brow becomes more apparent.

She's talking about more than just us. She wants to know what we do now that Sapphire and Stoner are free. It's a damn good question.

"I don't know," I answer honestly. "Slade and Brandie are running, and I guess we could go with them, if that's what you want." I stare out over the room as I speak but chance a quick glance at her to gauge her reaction. "Or we stay, build a life here and take things a day at a time."

"Part of me wants to run as fast and as far as I can. Sapphire and Stoner scare the hell out of me." She heaves a sigh and peers up at me from beneath her dark eyelashes. "You scare the hell out of me."

"I don't mean to scare you." The thought of her afraid of me feels like a knife is being shoved into my gut.

She waves her hand in a dismissive gesture. "Not like that. I mean, I know you won't physically hurt me. But emotionally?" She shrugs.

"What makes you think I would hurt you emotionally?"

"Jackson, you've had the love of your life already." She holds her hand up when my lips part to interrupt her. "No, let me get this out. I know you love me, but love isn't always enough. You've been saddled with me for months on end, and before we met, you were a widower still in love with his dead wife."

Ouch. That hurt.

"I don't think you'd ever intentionally break my heart, but are you sure you're ready to move on? Because I can't compete with your past." She shakes her head in frustration. "I won't compete with it, with them. I would never want you to forget them because they're a part of you, but I also don't want to spend the rest of my life coming in second."

I let her words sink in, along with the overwhelming panic that she's going to walk away from me, from us, without really giving me a chance. Sure, we've been together for months, like she said, but it's been under unusual circumstances. Maybe this is her way of telling me that what she feels, or felt, is just because of the situation and not because she's truly in love with me.

"Maybe you're right." Her gaze whips to mine. "Maybe it would be best for you to return to your place and I can have someone else keep an eye on you." The pain that flashes in her eyes levels me, but I stay the course. I can't take another loss so being the one to walk away is my only solution for self-preservation.

"But... you can't be—"

"It's been fun, really, but you've been through a lot and I'm no knight in shining armor. We did what we had to in order to get the job done, but it's done now. You should go live your life, find someone who makes you happy, who can give you what you deserve." I pick up her discarded beer, drain the bottle and slam it back on the bar. I lock eyes with her and force my next words past my lips. "That ain't me, darlin'."

Katelyn's eyes widen, and a sob tears out of her, as if it's coming from her soul. She shoves her fist against her mouth to stop the cries that follow, but it's impossible. I hurt her. I hate myself for it, but what else could I do?

Kill or be killed. Leave or be left. There are no guarantees in this life but the ones you give to yourself. And I just ensured that I won't be the one to get hurt later.

Who are you kidding? This fucking hurts.

Katelyn is trembling, and I want to reach out and hold her. I want to tell her I'm sorry and take the words back. I do neither of those things. Instead, I stare her down until she takes off running. I flinch as the door slams, punctuating her exit.

I stand there, frozen, for what feels like hours but is really only a few minutes. When I turn around, everyone's eyes are on me, judging me, chastising me. Unable to face the shitstorm that's no doubt going to come my way, I stalk toward the door.

A hand grips my arm and spins me back around. Slade's dark eyes drill a hole into me.

"What the fuck was that?"

"Nothing." I shake out of his hold.

"Didn't look like fucking nothing." Slade crosses his arms over his chest. He's standing with his feet braced apart, like he's ready to do battle, and that only adds fuel to my fury.

"Let it go," I demand.

"No." He shakes his head. "Jesus, Jackson. You fought me every step of the way about that girl." He points his finger at the door that Katelyn ran through. "I tried to warn you but you were too busy thinking with your dick."

"Don't," I growl. "Don't you dare talk about her like she's some slut that I used to get my rocks off."

"If the shoe fi—"

I grab him with both hands and fling him around and into the wall. My chest is heaving, and it hurts to breathe.

"You're pretty defensive about a girl you just let walk away." Slade quirks a brow at me, and I let him go. He brushes his hands down his shirt to smooth away the wrinkles I caused. "Listen, it's not hard. Do you love her?"

I think about his question. The answer is easy. Of course I love her. I nod.

"Good. Now, do you love her enough to fight for her? To let go of the past and prove to her that she's your future? To open yourself up to more pain? Because that's what this is.

You get that, right?" Slade can be a bastard, but he's a damn insightful one sometimes. *Asshole.* "You're so goddamn afraid of getting hurt again that you'd rather be the one to do the hurting. I've got news for you. Life hurts. Love hurts. People die, they leave. But every once in a while, a person comes along that's worth it because no one else in the world can make you feel the good like they can."

I hang my head. My heart threatens to beat out of my chest, sweat begins to bead on my forehead. The air is thick, and my lungs burn. Katelyn's gone. I pushed her away, and it physically hurts to acknowledge the fact that I may not be able to get her back.

Fuck!

32

KATELYN

"Hello?"

I glance at the clock on my nightstand and groan when I see it's almost three in the morning. I have a job interview at the elementary school tomorrow—correction, today—and answering calls from unknown numbers is not helping me get some much needed sleep.

"Just wanted to let you know we got here."

I'm glad I answered the phone when Brandie's voice comes through the line. It's clearer than the last time we talked, a week ago. My chest constricts when I think about that night. After I'd stormed out of the main house, I'd started to walk and quickly realized I had no idea where we were. Not really. About an hour into my fleeing, headlights had danced across the ground as a car pulled up beside me. It'd been Slade and Brandie. They drove me home in silence.

"Where's 'here'?" I ask.

"You know I can't tell you that." A muffled sound comes through the line, like she's covering the phone with her hand. Slade says something in the background, but I can't decipher the words. "Sorry. Um, we're safe. Slade's going to check in with his boss every week. I still can't believe they didn't make him take vacation for this."

"Really? That's good though. I mean, at least one of us still has the FBI on their side." My eyes well up at the fact that I don't. Jackson shoved me to the curb.

"God, Katelyn, I'm so sorry I got you into all of this."

"Stop. It's not your fault. Shit happens, right?"

Granted, it was some pretty crazy shit, but I mean it when I say it's not her fault. She couldn't have known what would happen.

"I guess."

"Are you going to be okay, Brandie? I hate that you're stuck with Slade. You barely know him and after what you went through…" I can't quite bring myself to finish that sentence.

"I'll be fine. Promise." Her voice cracks, and I know she's dangerously close to losing it. "Slade's an ass, but it's his job to protect me and he's too serious not to do his job."

An image of Jackson flashes in my brain. He's serious too, but that didn't stop him from getting involved with me. I almost hope that Brandie lets Slade past her walls. He seems like a decent guy, and he could be good for her.

Like Jackson was good for you?

"Listen, I hate to do this, but I have to get some sleep. I've got an interview in the morning."

"Oh, right. Okay."

"Call me tomorrow?"

"I, um… Slade says I can't call anymore. It's too dangerous, I guess."

"Right. Makes sense."

Brandie's ragged sigh curls around me, squeezes my heart. "Good luck at the interview."

"Thanks. Be careful out there."

"I will. I'll call when I can, if I can."

"'Kay."

"Bye, Katelyn."

"Later, Bra—"

The call disconnects before the words are out of my mouth. I hold the phone out in front of me, staring at the screen. I'm not sure how much more I can take. Losing Jackson has been awful, and now I have to lose Brandie, too? It's not fair.

I tap the green phone icon and navigate to my contacts. I scroll until I reach Jackson's entry and my thumb hovers over it. I want to call him, beg him to make the pain stop. I need to hear his voice. I need him to tell me that he loves me and that everything is going to be okay.

Before I can make that mistake, I toss the cell to my side and roll away from it. I punch my pillow and try to get comfortable again. Right now, I need sleep more than I need to make a fool of myself.

By the time the sunlight streams through the curtains and bathes my bedroom door in light, my eyes are heavy, gritty. Sleep never came, but I'm not surprised. I haven't slept more than three hours a night since returning to my apartment, and I'd gotten those hours in before Brandie called.

I throw the covers off of me and swing my legs over the edge of the bed. I'm beyond exhausted, but I need a job so I make my way to the shower and spend the next hour getting ready.

Once I'm dressed, in a black pencil skirt, white button-up blouse, and black blazer, I make some coffee and turn on the news. It's funny what trauma can do to a person. Before everything happened, I hated watching the news. It was always so depressing. Now, I can't stop watching.

The media hype surrounding the trial died down once the verdicts were made public, but things still felt far from over. As long as Sapphire and Stoner are free, I feel the need to know everything that's going on in this city and the news lets me do that. The meteorologist's voice drones on about the chances of rain today, and I make a mental note to grab my umbrella before I leave.

"Thanks, Bill." I scowl at the reporter's cheerful tone. I'm not a morning person, and she's too chipper for my liking. "In other news, the popular strip club, The White Lily, will have it's grand re-opening tonight. Sapphire Luciano and Gary 'Stoner' Jones were aquitted last week in the city's most high profile case of the year. At the time of their arrest, they were employees of The White Lily, and according to county records, they are now the new owners. Protesters have already started lining the streets…"

The rest of her words fade away as my coffee mug slips from my fingers and shatters on the floor. My ears are ringing and my vision is hazy. I try to suck in air, but it's too hard, too thick. How is this possible? I thought for sure they would leave the area, not stick around and re-open the club.

I stumble to the bathroom and fall to my knees in front of the toilet. My coffee makes a reappearance, but it isn't long before there's nothing left to purge. I lean back against the wall and focus on calming my shaky body.

After a few minutes, I'm steady enough to stand. I brush my teeth and make sure I still look presentable. I absolutely can't miss this interview. Not if I want a chance at something akin to a normal life.

Satisfied that I'm as ready as I can be, I go back to the kitchen. A glance at the microwave tells me I don't have time to clean up my mess, and I resign myself to cleaning it up when I get home. I grab my keys and cell phone, along with my purse, and walk out the apartment door, locking it behind me.

When I'm in front of the building, I press the unlock button on the keyfob and see the lights flash on the vehicle my parents loaned me. I'd always taken the bus and then Jackson had driven me everywhere, but he's gone and the bus makes me feel too exposed.

The hairs on the back of my neck stand up, making me second guess going anywhere alone. I glance up and down the street and see nothing out of the ordinary, so I climb in the front seat and start the engine.

As I pull away from the curb, I can't help but continuously checking my rearview mirror. I'm not a cop and not certain I'd even notice if I were being followed, but I can't help it. I glance at my cell phone, which I'd tossed into the center cup holder, and debate on calling Jackson. He'd know how to calm my nerves.

I manage to make it to the elementary school without incident and without caving into my fear. The interview goes well, and I'm told that I'll hear something by the end of the following week. I leave the school feeling lighter than I have in months. The position is perfect for me and even pays enough to make my student loan payments and other monthly expenses.

I stop by the grocery store to pick up a bottle of wine to celebrate—alone—and then run a few more errands before returning to my apartment. I toss my keys on the entry table and head straight for my bedroom to change. I search my cell phone for my music app and click on my favorite playlist, turning it up as loud as the little speakers will allow.

While John Legend's silky voice belts out the lyrics of his song, I shut my bedroom door behind me and set my phone on my dresser. I pull out my favorite black leggings and hoodie. I may be having a party for one, but no need to be uncomfortable. A creaking noise startles me and I rush to pause the music. Once the room is silent, it's exactly that. Silent. No creaking, no weird noises. Nothing.

Convinced I'm hearing things and being paranoid, I

unpause the song and finish dressing. I snatch my phone up and, singing along with the music, pull the door open. My words die in my throat as I come face to face with my worst nightmare.

"Hello, Kitty Kat."

I have no time to react because before I can stop her, Sapphire's fist connects with my jaw. My head whips to the side, and I feel a sharp prick in my arm. Cold liquid seems to flow from that spot and spread through my body.

"Not so big and bad without the fed, are ya?"

As whatever she pumped into me begins to take effect, my knees buckle and I fall to the floor. I hear Sapphire talking to someone, but I can't force my eyes open to see who it is and the drug is making it impossible to make out specific words.

She's right. Without Jackson I don't stand a chance. That's my last thought before the blackness drags me under.

33

JACKSON

"You've reached Katelyn. I can't come—"

I throw my phone at the wall. The sound of it shattering and falling to the hardwood floor provides little comfort. I've been trying to call Katelyn since I saw the news this morning, and every single time it's gone to voicemail. I tried, but I haven't been able to convince myself she's simply not answering because she doesn't recognize the number.

I stalk to my office at the back of the house in search of another cell phone. I was finally able to come home and completely leave Jack Duffy behind after the trial. I'd hoped Katelyn would be coming with me, but I'd fucked that up good.

I snatch a burner phone from the top drawer of my desk and call the most recent number I have for Slade.

"Who is this?" he answers on the fifth ring, and I send up a silent thank you to the phone gods.

"It's Jackson. Has Brandie—"

"You shouldn't be calling me."

"And you shouldn't still have this phone, yet here we are," I snap.

Slade heaves a sigh. I can hear a television in the background and it sounds like the news. I listen for anything that would give away their location, but it's not loud enough. It doesn't sit well with me that my partner is out there somewhere, handling Brandie on his own, but that's the way the boss wanted it.

"What's up?" he asks when silence ensues.

"Has Brandie talked to Katelyn?"

"She did last night. Why?"

"The White Lily is reopening tonight. It was on the news this morning." Slade curses under his breath. "I've been trying to get in touch with Katelyn all day, just to check on her, but she's not answering."

"Maybe she just doesn't want to talk to you after what happened."

"Yeah, maybe." I know he's right and that I'm probably overreacting, but I can't stop myself.

"Look, she was fine last night. Brandie even said she had a job interview today. I'm sure she's just busy."

"She had a job interview?" Jealousy whips through me that he knows something about her that I don't.

"Yep." Slade says something else, and it takes me a second to realize he isn't talking to me. "I gotta go. If you're really worried about her, go to her apartment. You should've gone a week ago anyway."

"That's none—"

The call ends, cutting my argument short. I walk to the window and look out over the acreage behind my house. Slade's right. I should just go to her apartment, make sure she's okay.

But then what? Walk away again?

I'm not sure I'd survive it a second time.

I step off the elevator and trudge down the hall to Katelyn's apartment door. I read the numbers on each door I pass until I reach number three eleven. I wrap my knuckles on the door and then shove my hands in my pockets as I wait. Glancing up and down the hall, I wince at the rundown decor. It's not a dump, but it's not the best either.

I knock on the door again and when there's still no answer, I call out to her.

"Katelyn, c'mon. It's Jackson." I pound on the wooden barrier. "I just want to make sure you're okay."

Still nothing.

I reach for the knob, and my stomach bottoms out when I find it unlocked. I reach for the gun in my waistband, grateful I thought to bring it. I open the door slowly and methodically make my way through the apartment. There's a set of keys on the table and her purse is next to it, along with an unopened bottle of wine. There's a broken mug on the kitchen floor and coffee splattered all over the place.

"What the hell happened here?" I mutter to myself.

A piece of paper on the front of the refrigerator catches my attention. I yank it from under the magnet and my blood runs cold.

Cats have 9 lives. How many more does she have to lose?

I'd worked with Stoner for a year, so I recognize his handwriting. I crumble up the note and toss it to the floor as I storm out of the apartment. I did this. I pushed her away and by extension, made her vulnerable.

As I race to The White Lily, I break every speed limit

there is. That's the only place she can be. No way would Sapphire and Stoner miss their own grand re-opening. A quick glance at the clock tells me I won't make it by the time the club opens, which may be for the best. Easier for me to sneak in that way.

I briefly debate on calling for backup but decide against it. The rage simmering through me rivals that of what I felt toward Kevin Vick so there's no telling what I'll do. No need to increase the witness pool.

I slam the car into park in the back lot and take a few minutes to think about my plan. I realize that I don't have one, other than to get in, get Katelyn, and get the fuck out. Good enough. I decide to enter through the main entrance, hoping that the new owners aren't stupid enough to keep any of the original staff. It'd suck if I were stopped before I even made it inside.

Luck is on my side, and I make it in without incident. I shuffle through the crowd, all the while looking in every direction for that familiar head of honey blonde hair. I also don't see Sapphire or Stoner, but that doesn't surprise me. Stoner is now part owner of the club so he's likely back in the office, and Sapphire is too vain to not be getting ready to tempt and tease the customers.

As I approach the door that leads to the back of the club where the offices are, the music starts to fade and the tap tap of someone testing a microphone registers. I whip around and see Sapphire standing on the stage. She's wearing stiletto heels and black leather straps criss cross her torso. Her nipples and crotch are exposed, and the crowd is going insane for her.

"Welcome to the grand re-opening of The White Lily!" The microphone amplifies her voice, but it's still difficult to make out her words over the cheers. "We are excited to announce a menu of extras for your sexual pleasure, along with a yearbook of sorts for you to choose the girl you want to play with. So, without further ado, get ready for a night you will never forget."

With that, she tosses the microphone to the side and the music kicks up to a bone jarring volume. Sapphire starts dancing, and the amount of attention she's garnering makes me sick. Men are throwing bills at her, no idea that they're supporting a level of crazy that would have their heads spinning. I narrow my eyes at her, and something off to the side of the stage catches my attention.

Stoner is watching, guarding, smiling. I want to go up on the stage and tear them both apart, but if they're out here, that means Katelyn is likely alone, or at least not guarded like Fort Knox. As I'm about to turn back to the door and go through, Sapphire looks in my direction and I can tell the moment she spots me because she freezes for a second before turning to Stoner and pointing at me.

No time to waste, I burst through the door and jog down the hall to the main office. The door is open, and the room is empty. My heartbeat skitters to a screeching halt as it hits me that I could be wrong about all of this. Then I remember the night I killed Vick and the conversation, if one could call it that, about Katelyn stripping. Sapphire hates Katelyn, so maybe she's planning something to knock her down a peg or two.

I retrace my steps and stalk toward the dressing room. Stoner barges through the door, and we stare each other down before I break the spell first. I glance to my left and see the fire alarm. A plan falls into place in the space of a few seconds.

I pull the alarm, hoping everyone in the club will scatter, including whoever is in the dressing room. I'm not disappointed when the door flies open and half naked chicks come out screaming. They all head right for Stoner, which gives me the little bit of time I need to slip in and slam the door closed behind me.

I flip the lock and slide the nearest dressing table in front of the door. I whirl around and sweep the room with my gaze. Katelyn isn't here. The fire alarm screeches around me, so I don't hear it at first. The shouting. The banging. When I do, I methodically search the room for it's source.

I reach Katelyn's old locker, and the sound intensifies.

"Katelyn?"

The yelling is unintelligible and intense. I need to get this locker open. There's a padlock on it, and I don't know the combination. *Fuck!*

"Katelyn, I'm gonna get you outta there. I just have to break the lock first."

I look around me for something, anything, that can get that accomplished. Nothing. Adrenaline surges through me. Someone is banging on the door to the room and shouting for me to come out. It's Stoner and he's fucking pissed.

Resigned, I lift my leg and kick the lock as hard as I can. The locker shakes, but the lock remains in place. Five more solid kicks, and the metal clangs to the floor.

I reach out and notice my hand shaking. Sapphire's voice mixes with Stoner's, and I know my time is running out. I throw open the locker, and I can feel as adrenaline is replaced by rage. The kind of rage that boils your blood and puts you in that killing head space.

Katelyn is in the locker, naked and crying. Blood oozes from a large gash on her forehead, and her jaw is an angry red and swollen. Her eyelids are drooping, but when they lock on me, a small smile forms.

"Ah, darlin', I'm so sorry." I gently pull her out and lift her into my arms.

"You came?" she mumbles when she lays her head in the crook of my shoulder.

A lump in my throat makes it impossible to respond. We can talk when I get her out of here. Leaving through the door isn't an option. Not with Sapphire and Stoner out there.

"You're only way out is through us," Sapphire screeches. *Speak of the devil.*

I search for another way out and realize that our only escape is through the window. We're on the first floor, so it's not too far of a drop, although the window is higher than most would be. I can't have Katelyn go first because she's not strong enough to catch herself, but the thought of leaving her inside, if only for a few seconds, has me wanting to vomit.

Knowing that's my only option, I set Katelyn down and help her to lean against the wall just under the window. I grab the nearest chair and launch it at the glass. The window shatters, and I know that I just gave away my plan. Speed just became priority number one.

"Open the fucking door! You know we won't let this go. We'll come after you." Stoner's tone is menacing, but I don't care. They won't get her.

I slide a chair under our escape route and step up onto it. I glance at Katelyn and hold my hand out for her to grab so I can help her up. When we're both on the chair, my arms gripping her tight, I lean in and give her instructions, praying she understands.

"I'm gonna climb out first. Katelyn, I need you to hold on to the window sill and pull yourself up and over so I can catch you on the other side." Her stare is blank. Shit. "Katelyn, do you hear me?"

She nods, but I'm not convinced. Maybe this isn't a good idea. She's too weak to hoist herself up. I thrust my fingers through my hair and rethink the plan. I'm going to have to help her out first, which means she may hit the ground hard and hurt herself worse, but at least she'll live.

"Okay, new plan." I grip her chin and force her to look at me. "Katelyn, you with me?"

She nods.

"Good. Okay. I'm going to help you through first. This window opens up to the alley where I took you that first night. You remember that?" Again, she nods. "I need you to summon every bit of strength you have so you don't fall too hard. Can you do that?"

When she nods, I waste no more time. I lift her up and watch as her head disappears through the opening. The jagged edges of the broken glass scrape alone her skin and blood drips down. She whimpers with every inch I shove her away from me.

"Put your arms out to brace your fall," I demand.

I give her one last push and the thud of her hitting the pavement is sickening. I reach up and pull myself through the window, ignoring the stabbing pain of the broken glass into my palms and across my stomach as I do. I'm dimly aware of the fact that the pounding on the door behind me is lighter, but no less urgent.

I see Katelyn on the ground, her arm at an impossible angle. She appears to be passed out, which is probably for the best. I do as I instructed her and stiffen my arms to brace for the fall. When I land, more pain ricochets through my body, but again, I ignore it.

"Where the fuck do you think you're going?"

I whip my head toward the voice, and Stoner's standing there, gun pointed at me. I slowly stand up, never taking my eyes off of him, and raise my hands. The metal of my gun digs into my back, reminding me that it's there, taunting me because I can't use it.

"You don't have to do this," I say, knowing full well he doesn't give a damn and even if he doesn't *have* to, he's just crazy enough to *want* to.

"We've got plans," Stoner replies. His voice is too casual, too calm. Psycho motherfucker. "Big plans. But we need Kitty Kat." He tips his head toward Katelyn.

I glance down at Katelyn's battered body and am shocked to see that she's moving around a little, coming to. I hear the distinct sound of Stoner's gun being cocked.

"We don't need you, though."

"You'll never get away with this."

Sirens split the air. Seems someone called 911 when I pulled that fire alarm, thank God. Stoner suddenly seems nervous, twitchy. Not good for a man holding a gun.

"You can run," I offer. "Run before they get here and don't look back. I won't say anything. Just let us go and run."

Stoner appears to be thinking about it but then his body tenses.

"I'm not a fucking pussy. I don't run when there's trouble." The vein in his neck bulges. "I finish the job."

"Do-don't," Katelyn mumbles from behind me.

"Shut up!" Stoner yells and shifts his aim to her. "I give the orders."

"I-I'll go wi-with you."

"The hell you will," I snap.

"Ja-Jackson, p-please."

"You're not fucking sacrificing yourself. Not for me."

"Would you two shut the fuck up?!"

Stoner's dangerously close to snapping. I need to end this, or at least keep him focused on me. Might as well go for broke. Before he can guess what I'm doing, I launch myself at him, knocking him to the ground. I land on top of him and begin to throw punches, one after another. He fights back and flings me off of him.

My breath whooshes out of me when I land on the cracked pavement. Gravel and whatever other nasty alley trash there is digs into my flesh and clings to my clothes.

Stoner straddles me and pummels my face and ribs. I'm not a small man by any stretch of the imagination, but Stoner is bigger and crazier. I find myself in a position where all I can do is try to block the blows.

Boom!

Stoner's eyes grow wide and the attack stops. He falls to the side, and a red puddle forms under his body. I kick at him to dislodge myself completely and scramble to my knees. My eyes dart to my right, and Katelyn's standing there, the gun dangling from her fingertips.

"H-he was going to k-kill you." Her face is pale and the weapon slips to the ground at her feet.

I glance back and forth between Katelyn and Stoner. I hate that she had to be the one to pull the trigger, but I'm glad she did. She saved me.

"J-Jackson?"

I rise to my feet and walk toward her. "Yeah, darlin'?"

"I th-think I'm g-gonna…"

Katelyn's knees buckle, and I rush forward to catch her before she can fall and do more damage. I lift her into my arms and carry her to my car. I could take her back inside and have her rushed to the hospital by whoever the sirens belonged to, but I don't.

She's my responsibility, and I don't trust anyone else to do what I can do myself. When I get to the car, I lay her down in the backseat. She moans but doesn't wake. I'll get her to the hospital come hell or high water. She's not dying today. And I'm never leaving her again.

I pushed Katelyn away out of self-preservation but I realize now how stupid that was. Losing my family the way I had was tragic and never should have happened, but I can't let the pain from that stop me from taking a chance on anything good now. I will always miss Melinda and Ben. I will always wish their lives hadn't been cut short by a madman. But they had.

They'll always hold a place in my heart, but they're my past.

Katelyn is my future. Whether she realizes it or not.

34

KATELYN

"When can I take her home, doc?" *Doc?*

"Her injuries aren't as severe as they appear on the surface." *Really? Feels pretty damn serious to me.* "I want to keep her for another night, just to be sure there are no complications, but I'd say, if all goes well, I'll discharge her tomorrow morning."

I open my eyes and peer at Jackson. He shakes hands with a man in a white coat, although he appears to be doing so gingerly.

"Thanks, doc."

"No problem. Now," the doctor takes a deep breath and releases it, "you really should go home and get some rest. Your injuries may not be severe, but they aren't nothing, either."

"I'm not leaving."

"Jackson," I croak. My throat is dry, my voice hoarse.

Jackson and the doctor shift their focus to me. The doctor steps up to my bed and checks my vitals, shines a light in my eyes. Jackson stands back and lets him do his thing.

"You've had a rough couple of days, young lady." The doctor—Dr. Lim, MD according to his white coat—is an older man and reminds me of my grandfather. His hair is grey and his eyes wrinkle at the corners when he smiles. He pats my hand. "But you'll be good as new in no time."

I try to speak, but nothing comes out. I point to the water and Jackson rushes forward to pour me a cup and walks to the other side of the bed. He brings the cup to my lips and helps me take a few sips. It dribbles down my chin, but I don't care. The cool liquid soothes my aching throat.

After Jackson pulls the cup away, I see him, really see him, for the first time. His face is bruised, and his nose is crooked. His shirt appears bunched, and when I glance down, I realize it's from bandages wrapped around his torso underneath the black material. He still looks like sin.

"You scared the hell out of me, darlin'."

"I'll leave you two alone."

The doctor shuffles out of the room, leaving a deafening silence behind.

"How long have I been here?"

"Two days." Jackson sits in the chair next to the bed and picks my hand up in his. "Two long fucking days."

"I don't... What... How did I get here?" My thoughts are jumbled. Memories come in short bursts. The moment I opened my apartment door. Something cold flowing through me. Seeing Jackson when he opened the locker. The alley.

"I brought you. After."

Jackson's eyes lock on mine as if he's willing me to remember. *After what?* I search my mind for the answer, and it slams into me like a freight train barreling down the tracks at warp speed.

"Stoner. I... I... he was going to kill you."

"Probably."

"I couldn't l-let him k-kill you." A sob tears out of me, from deep in my gut.

Jackson stands and climbs in the hospital bed next to me. He wraps me in his arms and holds me while I cry. In my heart, I know I did what I had to, but I killed a man. I ended a human being's existence and that's going to take a while to accept.

"Shh. You did nothing wrong." Jackson's breath skitters across my skin as he whispers in my ear. He brushes my hair out of my face. "It was him or me. You saved my life."

I cry until I have no tears left. I cry until the only thing I can do is sleep. When I wake up again, Jackson is still in the bed with me, his quiet snore like music to my ears. I grip his hand and squeeze, causing him to stir.

"Hi, darlin'," he mumbles.

"Hi."

I manage to roll over and face him. We stare at each other for a minute before we both speak at once.

"We need to talk."

"I'm so sorry I didn't protect you."

I laugh and it sounds hysterical to me. He chuckles and cups my cheek. Jackson leans forward and presses his lips to mine. The kiss is soft, tentative, like he's trying not to break me.

When he breaks the connection, I rush forward and kiss him with as much heat as I can muster. It hurts, but the pain is worth it.

Jackson kisses me back, and his tongue glides along my bottom lip. I suck it into my mouth, swirling my own tongue around it. Frustration wells in me that we're in a hospital bed and can't take this any further.

"We need to talk," I rasp out when the kiss ends.

Jackson's eyes are closed, but he nods.

"You pushed me away." The words are painful, raw, but true. And they need said. "You didn't want me."

"No, no, no." He leans his forehead on mine. "Katelyn, I was wrong. So wrong. I thought…"

"You thought what?" I ask when his words trail away.

He heaves a sigh. "I thought I'd just get hurt again, and I couldn't stand that possibility. So, yeah, I pushed you away."

I let his words swish around in my mind as I try to make sense of them. I get what he's saying, but it doesn't make it hurt any less.

"That was stupid," I pout.

"Yeah. It was."

"I need to know what you want from me, Jackson. If you're too scared to give us a shot, then walk away now."

"I'm not going to lie, I'm terrified." My heart cracks at his words. "But I'm more afraid of *not* trying then of what could possibly go wrong."

I lift my eyes to his, afraid of believing what he's saying.

"Katelyn, I thought I could push you away, forget about you. I was wrong. So fucking wrong."

"And what do you think now?" I hold my breath, waiting for his answer.

"I think I can't live without you." He presses a light kiss on my lips. "You were right, I'll never forget Melinda and Ben. They will always be a part of me. But you were wrong that you'd come in second. You don't need to compete with their memory. It wouldn't even be a fair competition. You'd win, every time."

"How can you be so sure?" The cracks in my heart are filling a little more with each word he utters.

"Because you're here. You're alive. They're my past. You're my future."

∽

Jackson pulls into a long, winding driveway and the house before me is one I don't recognize.

"Where are we?" I ask, confused. "You said we were going home."

"This is home, darlin'." Jackson cuts the engine and twists in his seat to look at me. "It's my *real* home." He ducks his head for a moment before pinning me with his stare. "And now it's yours."

"But I thought…"

"What? That we were going back to that ramshackle one story?" He barks out a laugh. "Katelyn, I was undercover. The house was part of that. I live here." He tilts his head toward the sprawling structure behind him.

I don't bother to mention my apartment. I'll have to do something with it eventually, but going back to it is out of the question right now. I let myself take in my surroundings and almost immediately, calm washes over me. Jackson clearly has acres of land because I don't see any neighbors, and the last house we passed had been a few miles back.

The house is two stories with lots of windows. It's got grey siding and a black metal roof, which is indicative of rural living. You'd never know we were so close to a major city. Not here. It's too serene, too green.

"Ready to go inside?" Jackson doesn't wait for my answer before climbing out of the car and coming to open my door.

I follow him to the steps and up onto the porch. There are two rocking chairs, and I can envision us sitting out here in the evening, a couple of dogs sprawled at our feet and kids playing in the yard.

Where had that come from?

"C'mon, I'll show you around."

Jackson laces his fingers with mine and tugs me inside. He's careful not to push too hard, as I'm still sore as hell. When we enter, my breath catches.

"Wow. This is amazing."

Jackson shrugs. "It's home."

"No, Jackson, this is incredible. And so you." I might not have known him long, but the rustic interior and leather furniture seem perfect for him. I turn in circles to take it all in.

"You can do whatever you want." My eyes dart to him and narrow in question. "I mean, this is your home now, too. I want you to be comfortable here."

He shoves his hands in his pockets and appears nervous, uncomfortable. It's adorable and completely unnecessary. I step closer to him and place a hand on his chest. His heart thumps wildly beneath my palm.

"Can I make a suggestion?" I bat my eyelashes at him. His heart beats faster as he nods. "Let's make it comfortable for both of us. If this is going to be *our* home, we both need to be happy."

His eyes light up, and I chuckle. I briefly consider that this might be way too much way too fast, but I don't care. We don't get to pick and choose who we fall in love with.

"I'm in love with you, you know that right?" I ask.

"I love you, too. So goddamn much," he says on an exhale.

No other words are necessary. We've got love and that's all that matters.

"Show me our room?" I purr.

"You sure? You're not too sore?"

He rubs his hands up and down my arms. He's right, I'm sore, really sore, but not too sore.

"Show me our room, Jackson," I demand.

He bends to scoop me up in his arms and carries me up the stairs. He's going too fast for me to take in anything we pass, so I make a mental note to get the rest of the tour later. Jackson lays me down on the bed and climbs his way up my body.

What follows is passionate, slow, sweet, and just what we both need.

EPILOGUE

JACKSON

One month later...

"Any news?"

Slade sounds frustrated, tired. This is only the second time we've talked since the night Katelyn killed Stoner and Sapphire got away. The White Lily was permanently shut down that night. The strippers were interviewed, and it was determined that there was more than stripping taking place.

"No, nothing." I rub the back of my neck. "Did you move again?"

"Yeah. We try to move every week or two." Slade heaves a sigh. "I'm not sure how much longer I can do this, man. And Brandie? She's struggling."

"I know. But until Sapphire is caught, she can't come back."

"But why do I have to be the one to protect her?"

"I remember you saying you wanted to. That you had to 'do the right thing,'" I remind him.

"Whatever."

"Look, it won't be much longer. The bitch will slip up and we'll get her. Just hang in there."

"You better."

"We will, I promise."

"Fine." I hear Brandie ask Slade if she can talk to Katelyn. She snaps at him when he says 'no', and I chuckle. He really does have his hands full with that one. "We're gonna have to let them talk sooner or later."

"We agreed. They can't talk until this is over. Too risky. What if Brandie lets something slip about your location? I'm fairly certain our calls aren't being traced or tapped, but no point in testing that theory."

"Yeah, yeah. So," Slade changes the subject. "Is today the day?"

"I don't know what you're talking about."

He chuckles. "Right. And I'm the president of the United States."

The front door slams, and footsteps echo off the hardwood floor.

"Katelyn's home. Gotta go."

I disconnect the call before he can respond and shove the phone in my pocket. Katelyn breezes into my office and has a smile on her face. It took me no time at all to get used to having her here, and we've done a lot to make this place ours instead of mine.

"How was your day?" I ask as she steps around my desk and wraps her arms around my shoulders.

"It was great. Remember that kid I was telling you about, Johnny?" When I nod, she continues. "He was able to finish his reading assignment today. For the first time, he got through it in the time allotted. You should have seen the look on his face."

Katelyn got the job she interviewed for the day she was kidnapped, and she loves it. Her students are everything to her, and seeing her face light up when she talks about their successes fills me up.

"That's great, darlin'." I stand up and turn to face her, her body leaning in to mine. "How 'bout we celebrate?"

"Mmm, what did you have in mind?" Usually we just hang out at home during the week, but this seems like too good of an opportunity to pass up.

"Nothing crazy. Bottle of wine down by the pond, picnic dinner, making out like teenagers." I nuzzle her neck and nip at the hollow of her throat. "The perfect night."

"I think I can get on board with that."

"Then let's go."

I turn my computer off and lead her out to the kitchen, where a picnic basket and a chilled bottle of wine are already waiting for us. I snatch up the blanket I'd set out beside it and tug her toward the back door.

"You already had this planned," she accuses, but there's no censure in her tone.

I shrug. "I have no idea what you're talking about."

"Jackson Stark, you just lied to me," she squeals, but again, there's no censure or anger.

"Katelyn Dawson, shut up and follow me," I joke.

She pouts but does as she's told. The sun hasn't set yet, but it's starting to dip. The weather is perfect. Minimal clouds, crisp fall air. When we reach the spot I'd picked out earlier, I spread out the blanket and start unloading the contents of the basket. Katelyn sits down and tips her head to the sky, taking in a deep breath. When her head lowers, there's a serene smile on her face.

"You're right. This is perfect," she murmurs.

Katelyn

Today has been incredible, and Jackson's romantic side is only making it better. I reach my hand up to grab his and pull him down next to me.

"I have something I want to tell you," I say.

"Me first."

He shoves his hand into his pocket, and when he pulls it back out, his fist is wrapped around an object, but I can't tell what it is. Jackson shifts to his knees and holds the object out in front of him. A black velvet jewelry box.

"Katelyn," he begins. "Before I met you, I was focused, single-minded, stuck in the darkness. Then you came along and it was like a portal opened up into another world, you were so bright. We've been through a lot, more than most. But that's only made us stronger. I can't promise that there will never be any bad times in the future. I've learned that the hard way. What I can promise is that I will stand by you through every one, and I will give you as many good times as I can in a lifetime." Tears are streaming down my cheeks as he talks. He brushes them away with his thumb before he swipes at his own. "I can't imagine a life without you in it. I don't want a life without you in it. Will you marry me?"

I don't even have to think about it. I launch myself at him, knocking him over onto his back. I rain kisses on his face, laughing and crying through it all.

"Is that a yes?"

"Yes. Yes, yes, yes. I will marry you."

He wraps his arms around me and rolls us over so he's straddling me. Somehow, he manages to disengage long enough to take the ring out of the box and slide it onto my finger. I hold my hand out in front of me to admire the sparkling diamond.

"I love you more than what should be legal," he says when he leans over me, bracing his hands on either side of my head.

I give him a smacking kiss, holding his head with my hands.

"We love you, too."

"Oh, thank G—" His eyes narrow. "Wait. What did you say?"

I smile through the tears. The happy tears.

"We love you, too."

"Does that mean what I think it means?"

I nod. He sits up and glances down at my stomach, still too flat to tell I'm growing a baby.

"Are you sure?" He asks when he returns his gaze to mine.

"Very sure. I had a doctor's appointment today and got it confirmed. That was the 'something' I wanted to tell you."

"We're gonna have a baby," he whispers with awe.

"Well, I'm going to have a baby. You're going to watch." I give him a wry smile.

"We're going to have a baby." He jumps up and whoops with joy. If he could, I've no doubt he'd climb to a mountaintop and scream it for the world below to hear.

"Yeah, Jackson, we're going to have a baby."

BONUS CHAPTER

Need more of Jackson and Katelyn? Sign up for my newsletter at andirhodes.com for an EXCLUSIVE bonus chapter, as well as updates on upcoming novels and giveaways.

SNEAK PEEK AT SLADE'S FALL

BOOK TWO IN THE BASTARDS AND BADGES SERIES

Slade...

As an FBI agent, I've sworn to uphold the law, to protect the public from the monsters of society. As a man, I've sworn off love and relationships. Multiple failed marriages have made me cynical and uninterested in anything beyond meaningless one-night stands. When an assignment puts me in close quarters with a feisty woman who's been victimized, I'm forced to question everything. She's a combination of infuriating sass and sexy as hell vulnerability, and I'm not the least bit confident in my ability to keep her in the 'just an assignment' category.

Brandie...

I've always been a bit of a wild child, a temptress of fate. That all comes to a screeching halt when I'm used to pay off my boss's debt. I'm held for months and forced to serve my new master. When I'm rescued, all I want to do is go home and try to live as normal a life as possible. Unfortunately, being rescued doesn't mean I'm safe. My life remains in constant danger, and I'm forced to rely on an FBI agent who pushes my buttons and makes me feel things in a way that should be impossible with what I've been through.

PROLOGUE

SLADE

"Motherfucker!"

The coffee mug sails through the air and shatters against the wall. Hot coffee splashes, hitting me on the back of the neck. I clench my hands into fists and count to ten, but the technique does little to cool the fury sliding through my veins. Although it's better than following through on my fantasy to strangle Brandie.

"Brandie, you've got two seconds to calm the hell down," I manage to grit out.

"Or what?" she snarls. "You're gonna keep me locked up in this stupid cabin? Oh wait," she cocks her hip and taps her finger next to her full lips, "I'm already trapped here."

"Look, I don't like it any more than you do, but I'm not your enemy."

"Coulda fooled me."

Brandie spins on the balls of her feet and stomps toward her bedroom, slamming the door shut behind her. I heave a sigh as the windows rattle and hang my head.

When Brandie and I left our lives behind, I'd told myself

it was the right thing to do. That I was protecting her. And it's the truth. I *am* protecting her.

But who's protecting you?

The question mocks me. I don't need protection. Certainly not from a pint-sized female with a smart mouth. *And a hell of a throwing arm.* I shake my head at the thought. I've had more things thrown at me in the last two months than bullets have been fired at me throughout my entire FBI career.

Brandie is infuriating. And sexy as hell. My safety isn't the only reason I want out of this assignment, because that's what it became when I opened my big mouth and offered to protect her… an assignment. I want out because my cock can't take much more.

When she's not launching objects at me, Brandie is actually fun to be around. Her smart mouth is appealing in ways it shouldn't be, and her body calls out to me on such a primal level that I'm not sure what to make of it. I just know that it's too much for any one man to handle.

I know that this has been hard on her, not to mention the shit she went through before we rescued her, but I'm not her enemy. Of course, moving locations every week probably doesn't make me her friend either. But I could be, if she would just let me.

I make my way toward her room intent on explaining, *again*, why I've set the rules I have. I haven't shown her the text I received from Jackson earlier, but maybe I need to. When I reach her room, I register the music she's got playing, and wonder what she's playing it on. It's not like we're in a permanent residence where she has a stereo, and I took her cell phone from her back when we left.

I wrap my fingers around the doorknob and heave a sigh when I find it locked. Of course it's locked. Why I thought it wouldn't be is beyond me.

"Brandie, c'mon, open up," I shout through the wooden barrier.

I'd force my way in if this weren't a rental. As it stands, we have limited short term options for places to stay, unless we stay in a hotel. Every once in a while, hotels are fine, but sometimes it's just nice to have a place with a kitchen and multiple bathrooms. For someone on the run, she's certainly managed to stockpile a shitload of girly shit. Make-up, hair products, lotions, and anything else you can think of are usually littered all over the bathroom counter within ten minutes of arriving at a new location.

I know we could stay in one of the safe-houses, but I've been hesitant to do that. The people I'm protecting her from likely have connections far beyond what the FBI is aware of, and I don't want to take the chance of the safe-houses being compromised. Maybe I need to consider it though, or at least take her opinion into account.

"Brandie, please, open the damn door."

I know she can hear me. Yes, there's music on, but it's not so loud that it drowns me out. I put my ear up to the door to listen for footsteps, and when I don't hear them, I start banging on the door, damages be damned.

"Jesus," she says on an exhaled breath as she yanks the door open. "What do you want?"

I had my words planned out, but they fly out of my mind when she's standing in front of me. She's wearing a T-shirt and panties, and while I've seen her in less, as in naked, there's something about the way she looks that barrels through me and hits me straight in the cock.

"Slade?" she asks when I remain silent.

"Hmm?"

"What the hell do you want?"

She cocks her hip and balances a slender hand at her

waist. I force my eyes to focus on her face, and it takes several tries before I can push words past my lips.

"Uh, we need to talk."

"Seriously? Because I'm pretty sure I've got nothing more to say to you right now."

"Shit," I mumble under my breath. "Look, can you please just put some fucking pants on and come out into the other room?"

She ignores my request for additional clothing and shoves past me. I roll my eyes and follow her, doing my best not to let my gaze fall to her ass and the sway of her hips. She bypasses all of the furniture and sits on the floor, cross-legged, which gives me a pretty spectacular view. I have to wonder if this is her intent or if she truly has no idea the effect she has on me.

"I know you think I'm controlling, but—"

She snorts and I glare at her.

"But, we're gonna need to find some common ground here." I pace the room as I speak. "I can't imagine what it was like for you when Luciano had you, but I'm not him and I want to keep you safe."

"You're right," she snaps. "You can't imagine. No one can."

Brandie had been given to Saul Luciano by Kevin Vick, both of whom had been the target of FBI and DEA investigations, as payment for a debt. Prior to that, Brandie was an escort, but regardless, she hadn't signed up for what she got. Drugged, probably raped, treated like a dog and held against her will. I helped with the bust that put Luciano in prison and ended with Kevin Vick's death. Unfortunately, Luciano has a daughter, Sapphire, and she's out for revenge.

There'd been another player in the game, Gary 'Stoner' Jones, but he's dead. My partner, Jackson, had been undercover and managed to fall in love with Brandie's best friend, Katelyn. After Luciano was sent to prison, his daughter and

Stoner purchased the strip club where Jackson and Katelyn met. Some shit went down and Katelyn shot and killed Stoner. While he's no longer a threat, his girlfriend is fucking pissed and out for blood.

When I read Jackson's text earlier, rage simmered just beneath my skin. Then Brandie asked if we could go do something, anything, to get out of the house. I'd panicked. Up until this point, we've been careful but there's always been the added security in knowing exactly where Sapphire is because Jackson has been monitoring her movement. That all changed this morning.

I lower myself to the floor to sit next to Brandie. We stare at each other for a long moment before she breaks eye contact and pulls her knees up to her chest and wraps her arms around them.

"Is there more to this conversation, or did you just want to bring up the one thing I can't talk about?"

"Stop it," I snap. "Why are you always trying to pick a fight with me? I'm not the fucking enemy here."

Her gaze swings to me, and there's a sheen in her eyes that has my stomach plummeting. Brandie doesn't cry, much, but when she does, it's usually uncontrollable and makes me feel helpless.

"You keep telling me you're not the enemy." She squeezes her eyes shut, and a tear rolls down her cheek. She takes a deep breath but makes no move to wipe away the wetness. With her eyes still closed, she whispers, "Deep down, I know you're not. I believe you and appreciate everything you're doing for me but…"

"But what?"

"It feels a lot like what they did." The words come out on an exhale.

Tears stream down her cheeks, unchecked and I can't stop myself from reaching toward her and wiping them away with my thumb. Her shoulders shake with sobs, and everything in me wants to wrap her up in my arms and promise her it'll be okay. But I can't do that. Not now. Not ever. This is a job, *she's* a job, and I need to remember that.

"I'm sorry that it brings back bad memories, but I promise you, I will never hurt you."

"Don't make promises you can't keep, Slade."

The way my name rolls off of her tongue is seductive, and my brain knows she's not meaning it to be but my dick doesn't get the memo. I shift to stand up and turn away from her so she can't see what she does to me. I wish boners came with an on and off switch because there are definitely times when it's inappropriate, but unfortunately, it's not something I can control.

When I glance back at Brandie, my anger threatens to explode. She has so much passion, so much fire in her that seeing her like this, scared, uncertain, puts chinks in my heart that I thought I'd long ago repaired. No one should have to experience what she did, and the turmoil it's caused for her makes the words I need to say that much harder.

I take a deep breath and force the words out, knowing there's no way around it and vowing to get her through whatever comes her way.

"Brandie, Sapphire managed to slip her surveillance."

ABOUT THE AUTHOR

Andi Rhodes is an author whose passion is creating romance from chaos in all her books! She writes MC (motorcycle club) romance with a generous helping of suspense and doesn't shy away from the more difficult topics. Her books can be triggering for some so consider yourself warned. Andi also ensures each book ends with the couple getting their HEA! Most importantly, Andi is living her real life HEA with her husband and their boxers.

For access to release info, updates, and exclusive content, be sure to sign up for Andi's newsletter at andirhodes.com.

ALSO BY ANDI RHODES

Broken Rebel Brotherhood

Broken Souls

Broken Innocence

Broken Boundaries

Broken Rebel Brotherhood: Complete Series Box set

Broken Rebel Brotherhood: Next Generation

Broken Hearts

Broken Wings

Broken Mind

Bastards and Badges

Stark Revenge

Slade's Fall

Jett's Guard

Soulless Kings MC

Fender

Joker

Piston

Greaser

Riker

Trainwreck

Squirrel

Gibson

Satan's Legacy MC

Snow's Angel

Toga's Demons

Magic's Torment

Printed in Great Britain
by Amazon